ATTACK OF THE
BAYPORT BEAST

READ ALL THE MYSTERIES IN THE
HARDY BOYS ADVENTURES:

#1 *Secret of the Red Arrow*

#2 *Mystery of the Phantom Heist*

#3 *The Vanishing Game*

#4 *Into Thin Air*

#5 *Peril at Granite Peak*

#6 *The Battle of Bayport*

#7 *Shadows at Predator Reef*

#8 *Deception on the Set*

#9 *The Curse of the Ancient Emerald*

#10 *Tunnel of Secrets*

#11 *Showdown at Widow Creek*

#12 *The Madman of Black Bear Mountain*

#13 *Bound for Danger*

COMING SOON:

#15 *A Con Artist in Paris*

HARDY BOYS
ADVENTURES™

#14 *ATTACK OF THE BAYPORT BEAST*

FRANKLIN W. DIXON

ALADDIN New York London Toronto Sydney New Delhi

ALADDIN
An imprint of Simon & Schuster Children's Publishing Division
1230 Avenue of the Americas, New York, NY 10020
First Aladdin paperback edition February 2017
Text copyright © 2017 by Simon & Schuster, Inc.
Cover illustration copyright © 2017 by Kevin Keele
Also available in an Aladdin hardcover edition.
All rights reserved, including the right of reproduction in whole or in part in any form.
ALADDIN and related logo are registered trademarks of Simon & Schuster, Inc.
THE HARDY BOYS MYSTERY STORIES, HARDY BOYS ADVENTURES,
and colophons are registered trademarks of Simon & Schuster, Inc.
For information about special discounts for bulk purchases, please contact
Simon & Schuster Special Sales at 1-866-506-1949 or business@simonandschuster.com.
The Simon & Schuster Speakers Bureau can bring authors to your live event.
For more information or to book an event contact the Simon & Schuster Speakers Bureau
at 1-866-248-3049 or visit our website at www.simonspeakers.com.
Cover designed by Karin Paprocki
Interior designed by Mike Rosamilia
The text of this book was set in Adobe Caslon Pro.
Manufactured in the United States of America 0117 OFF
2 4 6 8 10 9 7 5 3 1
Library of Congress Control Number 2016941959
ISBN 978-1-4814-6835-0 (hc)
ISBN 978-1-4814-6834-3 (pbk)
ISBN 978-1-4814-6836-7 (eBook)

CONTENTS

Chapter 1	Step Right Up	1
Chapter 2	My Brother, the Skeptic	9
Chapter 3	Watcher in the Woods	21
Chapter 4	The Expedition	27
Chapter 5	The Benefactor	35
Chapter 6	Minor Adjustment	40
Chapter 7	Signs of Life	44
Chapter 8	Sighting	52
Chapter 9	No Joke	55
Chapter 10	Another Minor Adjustment	59
Chapter 11	The Beast Lives	68
Chapter 12	Trapped	75
Chapter 13	More Signs	81
Chapter 14	In Deep	86
Chapter 15	Brother Trouble	91
Chapter 16	Incoming!	95
Chapter 17	Outgoing	103

STEP RIGHT UP

1

FRANK

S JOE AND I MOVED THROUGH THE crowd, I spotted Spiderman chatting with Superman. Off to the right, a Jedi Knight ate a hot dog next to Captain America. We stopped short as Darth Vader marched across our path, his long black cape flowing behind him.

Just then, a beastly arm entered my field of view. Dark hair dangled in clumps from the appendage. Bony fingers stretched wide as they reached for the back of Joe's neck. Each fingertip ended in a sharp, jagged talon.

Instinctively, I opened my mouth to warn my brother, but then I caught myself. Hey, it had been his idea to drag me here, so . . .

The claws clamped onto my brother's neck. He jumped and spun around, eyes wide.

"Another victim of the beast!" said Hector Cruz—friend, practical joker, and owner of the beastly arm.

A grin spread across Joe's face. "Where'd you get that arm?"

Hector jutted a hairy thumb over his shoulder. "The lady at that cosplay booth let me borrow it."

"Of course there's a cosplay booth here," I muttered. Cosplay, or costume play, refers to the practice of people dressing up as their favorite comic book, TV, or movie characters. Not only were cosplay hobbyists everywhere, but all morning I'd taken photos of Joe and Hector standing with Wolverine, Batman, and Robocop, to name a few.

"Way cool," Joe said as he doubled back toward the booth filled with fanciful costumes.

"Maybe they have one of those new Stormtrooper helmets." Hector nudged me on the shoulder. "That would be sick, huh?" He hurried to catch up to Joe.

I sighed and trudged after them. "Yeah, real sick."

The entire morning had been my brother's big idea. You can bet *I* didn't want spend the first day of summer vacation at a sci-fi and cryptozoology convention. The science fiction part I could get behind. The cryptozoology part . . . not so much.

Cryptozoology. A made-up word describing the made-up science of studying made-up animals. At least, that's how I thought of it. But from the number of attendees and vendors at the convention, a lot of people seemed to take it very seriously. Many of the vendors had booths filled with retro action figures and comic books, but there were just as many selling Nessie statuettes. Nessie—better known as the Loch Ness Monster—is the mythical plesiosaur that, according to believers, somehow survived the mass extinction of dinosaurs sixty-five million years ago and is alive and well, swimming in a murky Scottish lake. I even saw a booth offering little chupacabra plush dolls. Why would any kid want to snuggle up to a Puerto Rican monster that's famous for living off goat blood?

Most of the crypto-vendors sold merchandise related to the main star of cryptozoology—Bigfoot. Posters, figurines, and dolls of the mythical apelike creature were everywhere. One vendor even had an eight-foot-tall, hairy replica that you could pose for photos with.

Bigfoot was the reason why this particular convention was held in Bayport at the beginning of every summer. Some people think that Bayport has its own version of the creature roaming the national forest outside of town. These believers even came up with a unique name for it: the Bayport Beast.

I caught up to Hector and my brother at the cosplay booth. Hector had indeed found one of the new Stormtrooper helmets among the many costumes from various science fiction and fantasy movies. He slipped it over his bushy brown hair. "Aw, yeah," came his muffled voice from inside the helmet.

"Here, try this," said the owner of the booth, a woman

decked out in full Klingon regalia. She looked exactly like one of the aliens from *Star Trek*, from the special-effects makeup and forehead ridges to the wicked dagger hanging from her belt. The woman reached a gloved hand over the counter and flipped a switch on the side of the helmet.

"What was—" Hector began. His voice crackled through a tiny speaker on the side of the helmet. "Oh. Cool!" He gave a quick glance around. "Lord Vader isn't here, is he? I'm mostly out of uniform."

"I thought we were trying to find Benny," I said.

"His booth is around here somewhere." Joe shrugged. "We'll get to it."

Hector cocked his head at us. "This isn't the booth we're looking for," his electronic voice murmured, impersonating someone under the influence of a Jedi mind trick.

Joe laughed. I shook my head.

"Okay, are you shopping or just playing?" the Klingon woman asked, hands on hips.

Hector removed the helmet. "Just playing," he admitted as he handed over the sci-fi headgear. "Little too pricey for me. Sorry."

I followed Joe and Hector as they made their way down the long aisle of vendors. I felt like I was babysitting two toddlers who were distracted by every toy they came across.

Joe examined a blue-and-red Transformer action figure from one of the tables and handed it to me. "Didn't you used to have this one when we were little?"

I nodded. "Yeah." I set the toy back on the table. "Optimus Prime . . . and you broke it."

Joe's eyebrows rose. "That's right." He reached for his back pocket. "Want me to buy you this one? To replace it?"

I ignored the question along with my brother's empty gesture. "I thought you were more interested in the cryptozoology than the sci-fi."

Joe moseyed past the line of booths. "Oh, I am. But you have to admit, this is cool stuff, right?"

"Yeah, the sci-fi stuff is cool. But there's a reason cryptozoology doesn't have its own convention. Because it's *all* sci-fi, if you ask me."

Hector caught up to us. He nodded in my direction. "Is he going off again?"

Joe rolled his eyes. "You know it."

"I thought you two were detectives," Hector said. "What's a bigger mystery than Bigfoot?"

I threw up my hands. "There's no mystery, because it doesn't exist."

Hector was right about one thing: we were detectives. My brother and I have been solving mysteries since we were kids. And not just kid stuff like finding missing pets; we've caught some major crooks in our time.

Hector squinted at me. "What about all those Bigfoot-hunting reality shows?"

"Just because it's called *reality* doesn't mean it's real," I replied. "And do you know how I know that those particular shows aren't real? Because none of them provide solid proof that Bigfoot exists. If they did, it would be on every news channel and burning up the Internet before they could even air the episode."

Joe threw an arm over my shoulder. "Listen, bro. You know I'm a logical person." I raised an eyebrow.

"*Mostly* logical," he corrected himself. "And I know there's a slim chance that these creatures actually exist. But don't you think the world would be a little more interesting with the possibility that they *might* exist?"

"I'm with Joe on this one," said Hector. "Bigfoot, Nessie, ghosts, aliens . . . it could happen."

I raised my hands. "Oh, I never said aliens didn't exist."

Hector did a double take. "Wait a minute. You don't believe in Bigfoot, but you think little green men are real?"

I rolled my eyes. "No, I don't believe in little green men. But just think about it. . . ."

"Here we go," said Joe.

"Our solar system is one of billons in our entire galaxy," I explained. "There are more than one hundred billion galaxies in the known universe. Mathematically, it's nearly impossible that we are the *only* planet in the universe with life on it."

"So, life on other planets?" Hector asked.

"Statistically? Highly probable," I replied with confidence.

"But little green men at Area 51?"

I shook my head. "Please."

We turned down the next aisle and found our friend Benny Williams standing behind a booth for Bayport's own Triple B Comic Shop.

"Hey! You guys made it," Benny said as we approached. He was about a foot shorter than us and almost seemed lost behind the racks of comic books on either side of him.

Benny was a huge fan of the Bayport Beast. He always had news of the latest sighting or the most recent theory, and he could prattle on forever about the Native American legends describing a giant fur-covered man who roamed the forest. According to local lore, early American colonists spotted the strange creature in the woods, and the town's founders named the beast.

As long as we'd known Benny, the beast had been his main hobby, bordering on obsession. So much so that he even had his own nickname.

"Benny the Beast!" Hector said. "How's it going?"

"Great," Benny replied. He moved down to the far side of the display table. "Check out my new Bayport Beast merch." He proudly gestured toward a small display of Bayport Beast caps, T-shirts, and sketches. "Everything a fan of the beast could want or need!"

Joe stuck a cap on his head. "I'm down for one of these."

While Benny rattled through his stock, I noticed another attendee taking interest—a tall, thin man in a blue blazer. He had a bandage on his forehead and a crazy spiked hairstyle that looked as if it had taken a half a tube of hair gel to create. I tried to decide if he was dressed as an obscure sci-fi character. One of the old *Doctor Who* doctors, maybe?

Hector held up an *I Saw the Bayport Beast* shirt. "This is cool. But I can't wear it if I haven't *seen* the beast, right?"

"Well, that might be about to change," Benny said.

"What do you mean?" I asked.

Benny reached into his pocket and pulled out a folded piece of paper. He spread it open, and I realized it was an old trail map for the local national forest. There were several dark *X*s drawn on different parts of the trails.

"I'm thinking about giving tours on all the latest squatch sightings," Benny explained.

Benny liked calling the creature a "squatch," short for Sasquatch, the name Native Americans gave Bigfoot back in the day.

"I've always wondered how you know about all the latest sightings," Joe said. "Where do you get your intel?"

Benny grinned. "I have my sources. Anyway, are you guys up for a campout as a test run?" He looked at us expectantly. "Free of charge, of course."

"Count me in," said Hector. He exchanged a fist bump with Benny.

Joe grinned and looked at me.

I slowly shook my head. "No, no, and no."

MY BROTHER, THE SKEPTIC

THE SKEPTIC

2

JOE

A COOL BREEZE WHISTLED THROUGH the trees the next morning as the sun climbed higher in the sky. I followed Benny and Hector as we hiked up a wooded trail. Each of us wore a backpack and used a hiking stick to navigate the steep path. Benny's huge backpack nearly dwarfed the little guy, but he seemed to be doing fine.

Most of the surrounding forest didn't resemble the enchanted woods in the Lord of the Rings movies. Thorny bramble vines and thick bushes covered much of the ground. The leafy canopy above us blocked most of the sun and created deep shadows, with only occasional shafts of light poking through. In places you couldn't see more than ten feet into the foliage. Even though miles of well-worn hiking trails cut through the dense forest, this was the perfect creepy setting for a beast hunt.

I glanced over my shoulder to glimpse Frank bringing up the rear. He seemed to be enjoying himself too.

Did I think I'd be able to convince my brother to join us on a Bigfoot hunt? Of course not. But talking him into camping with friends wasn't so hard.

For as long as I can remember, the Hardy brothers have been divided into two camps as far as sports were concerned. I've always excelled at team sports like soccer and baseball. Meanwhile, my older brother is better at adventure sports like kayaking and rock climbing. That's not to say I don't like camping. We both belong to our school's Green Environment Conservation Club, after all.

Either way, knowing how Frank geeks out about nature, I was sure it wouldn't take much of a nudge to get him to camp. And if some of us happened to be looking for the Bayport Beast along the way, so be it.

Up ahead, Benny stopped and held up a fist. Hector and I halted and remained still as Benny peered around us into the dense woods. Frank eased up beside me.

"How many times is he going to do that?" Frank asked.

"Give him a break," I whispered. "This is his first Bayport Beast tour, after all."

Frank shrugged and reached for one of the water bottles on the side of his pack.

"Last year, on this very spot, a family of four spotted the beast crossing the trail in front of them." Benny pointed to the trail ahead. "The creature disappeared over that small rise. It was the last sighting of the summer."

Benny hiked up the hill. When we joined him atop the rise, he continued, "Some people say the beast likes to be close to people, almost as if it wants to be part of a pack. Yet still it stays hidden. Always watching."

He turned to face each of us, then scanned the thick woods. "In fact, it could be watching us right now."

Benny stepped off the hiking trail to our right, ducking under some branches as he maneuvered down a narrow game trail. Game trails were much smaller, sometimes nearly imperceptible paths usually created by wildlife.

"Uh, if the beast could be so close, shouldn't we stay on the main trail?" Hector asked. "Besides, we could get lost."

"Don't worry," I replied as I made my way behind Hector. "I'm sure Frank has a compass."

"Of course I brought a compass," my brother mumbled behind me. "Didn't everyone?"

We snaked through the dense woods single file until the game trail led to a small clearing, where we found Benny studying a patch of tall grass.

"See how the grass is matted down like that?" Benny asked. "Looks like a squatch nest." He bent down and placed a palm in the center of the circular pattern. "One could've spent the night here."

"Whoa," Hector whispered as he knelt beside Benny. "Do you see any tracks?"

Benny shook his head. "Too much vegetation for its feet to make an impression."

"Too bad," said Frank. "Because then you might see some deer tracks. They bed down in tall grass like this."

I glanced around the ring of thick trees. "What else are we looking for?"

"See if there is fur snagged on any of the branches or bushes nearby," Benny directed. "And maybe look for some squatch scat."

"Some what?" asked Hector.

"You know, Sasquatch poop," Benny explained.

"Really?" Frank raised an eyebrow. "And what exactly does 'squatch scat' look like?"

Benny shrugged. "I don't know. But a squatch is big so I'm guessing something . . . substantial."

"Everything poops, right?" I asked. " Besides, *something* spent the night here. Maybe there are some clues as to what it was."

We searched the small clearing but came up empty. Then we made our way back through the thick forest and onto the main trail to continue our trek.

I understood why Frank was being such a pain about the whole Bayport Beast thing. He doesn't believe in cryptozoology at all. But being a detective, you think he'd be a little curious as to why people all over the world seem to catch glimpses of these creatures.

We followed Benny to two more locations on his map and even another "squatch nest." Each time, Frank was quick to point out a logical explanation for what the sighting could've been: a glance at a bear through dense underbrush, somebody in a gorilla suit. Frank had an answer for everything.

We stopped for lunch on top of a hill along a wide bend in the trail.

Benny took a long pull from his water bottle. "Just think, guys. The beast is out there somewhere."

"Benny . . . ," Frank began.

"Give the man a break," I told my brother. "This is why we're here."

Frank pointed at me. "This is why *you're* here. I'm just camping with some friends."

"That's okay," said Benny. "I bet you'll be a believer before we're through."

Frank threw up his hands. "What about a body?" he asked. "This thing can't live forever. Just think, if these creatures had been roaming the woods for so long that the original Native Americans had a name for them, then there had to have been several of them. Maybe a whole pack."

Benny gave Frank a suspicious look. "Yeah . . ."

"Then why hasn't anyone found a dead one?" Frank asked. "Everything dies, right? You'd think someone would've stumbled upon a Sasquatch skull at some point."

"A satchskull?" I asked.

Benny ignored my joke. "There aren't bear skulls lying

around either, and we know those exist."

I had heard Bigfoot hunters on TV use the same argument. They claim that big animals that die natural deaths quickly decompose or are eaten by scavengers, so it's rare to find their remains. I didn't know if it was true, but it sounded plausible.

"We know bears are real because they *are* real," said Frank.

"Sasquatches could bury their dead," Hector suggested. "Like people."

"Really?" Frank asked.

Hector shrugged. "Just saying."

"It makes sense," I added. "They could use satchshovels. Okay, not funny."

Frank smirked and rolled his eyes. I almost got a laugh out of him.

Benny grinned and pointed at my brother. "You just wait, Frank Hardy. We're not leaving until we spot the beast."

We hiked for a couple more hours, winding around the forest's many trails. Benny consulted his map and told stories of how hikers and campers either caught a fleeting glimpse or came face-to-face with Bayport's own Bigfoot. We spotted a few more hikers, and Frank even saw a red-tailed hawk perched on the branch of a large oak. However, we did not see anything resembling the Bayport Beast.

When the trail crossed an open field, Benny pointed to the other side. "In 1972 a hunter named Joseph Carroll spotted the beast near the tree line over there. That was back when you could still hunt here."

Benny led us to the other side of the field. "Carroll claimed to have shot the beast before it ran away. But he couldn't find the body or even a blood trail."

"Maybe he wasn't such a good shot," I said.

When the trail reached a dry creek bed, Benny stopped again. "In the summer of 1987, a young couple named Barry and Heidi Smith came upon the beast near that bank over . . . there." He pointed to a spot on the opposite side of the dry creek. "This time, the beast chased them up this trail for almost a mile before finally leaving them alone."

"Whoa!" said Hector. "That thing will chase you?"

"Some people have claimed that," Benny replied.

I glanced at Frank, who merely shrugged. I was glad he'd finally quit coming up with logical explanations for every sighting. He seemed to have decided to let Benny enjoy playing tour guide.

Benny finished by leading us to the summit of another hill.

"And now we'll camp at the very spot where it all began." Benny slipped out of his oversize pack. "This is the site of an early reported beast sighting—one of the first sightings ever."

"No kidding?" asked Hector.

"Wasn't it a mountain man or something?" I asked.

"Yeah, a fur trader named Ezra Winslow," Benny explained. "Winslow saw what he thought was another mountain man moving through the woods."

"Since wearing fur was no big thing to those guys, huh?" I asked.

"Right," agreed Benny. "He called out to the figure, but it wouldn't stop. When Winslow finally caught up, the beast turned around and scared the heck out of him."

"I bet it did," said Hector. He glanced at the dark woods. "I'm getting a little freaked out myself."

"Winslow dropped his musket and ran all the way back to his camp," Benny continued. "The next day he came back with others and searched this very spot. They didn't find any sign of the beast. But they did find Winslow's musket . . . snapped in half."

"Well, that's a clue," I said.

"Not really," said Benny. "Everyone thought Winslow broke it himself. No one believed his story."

"I wonder why?" asked Frank. He removed his pack and handed it to me. "You set up the tent. I'm going to grab some firewood."

"How come I have to set up the tent?" I asked.

Frank began counting on his fingers. "One: I drove us here. Two: you dragged me to that convention yesterday. And three: you have me hunting something that doesn't exist."

I shrugged. "Fair points." Hector and Benny smiled as Frank trudged off into the woods. "Don't worry," I told them. "He's really having a great time."

By nightfall, we had our tents set up, a campfire blazing, and stomachs full of roasted hot dogs and canned beans. Frank had even lightened up as the conversation turned away from the beast and toward our usual topics—sports, girls, and funny things that had happened at school last year.

"Why are you so into the Bayport Beast, anyway?" Hector asked Benny, breaking the unofficial conversational Beast Ban.

Benny grinned. "Frank's not going to believe me, but I saw it once."

I sat up straight. "For real?"

"Oh, yeah." Benny's eyes lit up. "I was camping with my family when I was eight. One night I took my flashlight and stepped away from camp to, you know, answer the call of nature . . ."

Frank and Hector laughed.

Benny continued. "Well, after I was done, I heard these footsteps in the woods. Not animal footsteps, human footsteps. Something on two legs creeping through the brush. And the footsteps sounded like they were coming closer and closer to me."

Frank sighed. "Deer can sound like a person walking through the woods."

"Dude, really?" I asked.

Frank held up both hands. "So can an armadillo. Just saying."

"He's right," said Benny. "But it wasn't either of those. Because when I finally got the courage to point my flashlight in that direction, I saw it."

"The beast?" prompted Hector.

Benny winced. "Well, kinda."

"What do you mean, 'kinda'?" asked Frank.

"Well, I was just a kid," said Benny. "I wasn't as tall as I am now. I spun my flashlight around and only caught the beast's legs."

"That's it?" asked Hector. "Why didn't you shine your flashlight up?"

"Because I was just a kid!" repeated Benny. "As soon as I saw those hairy beast legs, I ran back to camp and told my parents. My mom and dad returned with me, but we didn't see anything." A serious expression came over Benny's face. "I don't know if they really believed me, but I know it was real."

"Wow," said Hector.

I glanced at Frank, using all my sibling telepathy to get him to keep his mouth shut.

"Cool," was all he said. "I can see why that encounter would spark an interest." It was a diplomatic answer—sympathetic yet noncommittal.

"Aren't you going to tell me it was a bear or something?" Benny asked.

Frank raised his hands. "Hey, man. I wasn't there. I have no idea what you saw."

Benny's eyes narrowed. "I know what I saw."

I pointed to the map in Benny's lap. "Where did it happen?" I asked, trying to quash any skirmish before it started.

Benny happily unfolded the map and showed us a large *X* marked over a cluster of campsites near the trailhead.

An hour later, the fire had died down to glowing coals and we climbed into our tents: Benny and Hector into one and Frank and me into the other. As Frank unzipped his sleeping bag, he gave me a knowing glance.

"You know Benny only saw a bear, right?" he whispered.

"Probably," I agreed. "Benny is lucky he wasn't bear chow."

We didn't say anything else about it. Not only were the tent's walls paper thin (I could hear Benny and Hector's muffled conversation a few feet away), but I was also beat. From the sound of Frank's immediate snoring, it seemed to be the same for him. He sounded like he fell asleep as soon as he was zipped inside his bag. I drifted off too, in spite of my brother's droning snore in my left ear.

The next morning Frank and I split up from the others. We hiked the trails until we came upon a pair of abandoned dirt bikes. It was time to take our beast hunt to the next level! We each hopped on one and soon trees raced by as we tore through the forest. We flung fantails of dirt as we skidded around hairpin turns. We soared high into the air as we jumped over rises.

As we emerged into a large clearing. I caught movement in the distance. A tall, dark figure stood just outside the tree line—the Bayport Beast!

The creature raised two long arms, bared rows of sharp teeth, and charged toward us. Both of us hit the brakes and jerked our bikes around. The beast hurtled closer. I twisted the throttle and my bike bolted forward as I poured on the speed. Up ahead, Frank had the same idea.

Unfortunately, my front tire hit an obstacle. I didn't see what it was because I was too busy flying through the air—this time, without the dirt bike. I heard my bike crash behind me as I tumbled across the hard ground. The throttle must've been jammed, because the engine revved louder. When I rolled over, I saw the beast looming over me. It bared its jagged teeth again as it reached a bony hand toward my face.

I started awake, breathing heavily. I stared up at the dark tent ceiling and marveled at my realistic dream. I could still hear the deep warble of my dirt bike.

Only it wasn't a dirt bike. Was Frank snoring again?

"What's that noise?" Frank whispered.

As the sound grew louder, I realized that a human wasn't making it; it was wet and guttural, as if an elephant seal was getting ready to break into song.

"A bear?" I hissed.

"No way," Frank replied, though he didn't sound confident.

The noise grew louder, as if whatever was making it was moving closer.

"Come on," I said, unzipping my sleeping bag. I fumbled for my flashlight but couldn't find it.

"Aw, man," Frank hissed. "My bag's zipper! It's stuck."

My hand finally found my flashlight and switched it on. That's when the tent shook around us; something seemed to be pushing on the roof and at the sides.

Something—or *someone*—was trying to get in!

WATCHER IN THE WOODS

3

FRANK

OME ON, COME ON," I MUMBLED. THE zipper on my sleeping bag wouldn't budge. Something was pushing in on the thin fabric of our tent, trying to get through, but we couldn't tell what.

At first I thought it was a bear. It made the most sense, even though we had taken precautions by keeping our food strung up high in a tree. But this didn't sound like any bear I'd ever heard. Plus, bears roar when they're trying to fend off an attack, not when they're scavenging for food.

The zipper finally came free and I exploded out of my sleeping bag. We had to get out of there. Joe had the tent flap unzipped by the time I grabbed my own flashlight.

"Ready?" he asked.

"On three," I replied.

"Three!" Joe shouted as he dove out of the tent.

I was right behind him, rolling to a stop and jumping to my feet. Sticks and pinecones jabbed my socks, but I didn't care. We had to get some distance between ourselves and the bear.

When we were about twenty feet away, we stopped and aimed our flashlights back at the tent. Before our beams landed, though, I heard laughter.

"Hey!" Joe shouted.

Benny and Hector hovered over our tent. Hector had his hands on the ridgepole while Benny had his arms full with what looked like a coffee can.

Joe doubled over, catching his breath. "What the heck . . ."

"That was awesome!" Hector shouted. "You guys should be on the track team!"

"Thought the beast had you, huh?" asked Benny.

I marched back to the tent. "I thought it was a bear." I pointed to the stuff in Benny's arms. "What's that?"

Benny shifted to reveal a coil of thick rope on the ground beside him. One end jutted through a hole in the bottom of an extra-large coffee can. "I learned this in summer camp. All you need is a wet rope and a coffee can." He pulled the rope through the hole, and a wet growl reverberated out of the metal can.

"Cool," Joe said as he joined us.

I rounded on him. "Really?"

Joe waved me off. "Hey, they got us." He laughed. "I'm just sorry I didn't think of it first."

My lips tightened. "Is this part of the tour?"

Benny shrugged. "I don't know. Probably not."

Hector pointed at me. "That was just for you, man."

I shook my head and sighed. "Fine. You got us." I moved past them and crawled into our tent. "I'm going back to sleep."

"What's with him?" I heard Hector ask from outside.

"Frank's serious about his sleep," Joe replied.

I climbed back into my sleeping bag as they continued to chat it up outside. I was so irritated by the prank that I didn't expect to fall asleep for a good hour. But I was fast asleep before Joe finally made it back to the tent.

The next morning, it was cold Pop-Tarts and juice for a quick breakfast before we set out. The conversation on the hike back went pretty much the way it had the day before, except this time I kept quiet. Everyone seemed to understand that I wasn't thrilled about the prank, and I was content to follow along behind the rest of the group.

The only one who didn't understand why I was so irritated was . . . me. I've been on the receiving end of plenty of practical jokes (it's hard to avoid that kind of thing with a brother like mine); I've even pulled a few myself. So I couldn't figure out why this one bothered me so much.

After more hiking, it dawned on me. Last night, for a moment, I'd actually entertained the idea that the Bayport Beast might exist. For that fraction of a second, all logic went out the window and I was a believer.

I sighed. I guess I wasn't annoyed with Benny and

Hector; I was annoyed with myself. That's one of the bad things about self-reflection; sometimes it makes you realize just how big of a jerk you're being.

Up ahead, the guys were almost out of sight. They rounded a bend and then disappeared over a rise. I quickened my pace down the trail. Lucky for me, my backpack wasn't as full of food anymore, plus, we were hiking downhill, which made it easier. I figured I'd be able to catch up to them in no time.

Just then I caught movement out of the corner of my eye. Gazing into the woods, I stopped moving and slowed my breathing. I always enjoyed catching glimpses of wildlife and was quite good at spotting even the tiniest creature through dense foliage. But I didn't see anything among the trees.

I'd started walking again when this strange sensation crept over me; the feeling of being watched. I stopped and stared into the forest once more. Nothing.

A twig cracked.

I snapped my head to the side, following the direction of the sound, and peered through the greenery. There was nothing there.

As I began to turn back around, I caught the slightest motion out of the corner of my eye.

Peeking out between clumps of dense vegetation, about twenty feet away, were two eyes. My skin prickled when I realized that they were staring back at me.

"Has to be a bear," I whispered. The animal was hidden

behind so much vegetation, all I could see were its eyes and a hint of dark fur.

I'd seen a few bears before in these very woods. There are a lot of them around. They pretty much leave you alone if you leave them alone, slowly back away, and let them go about their bear business.

But a bear has a face that looks like that of a big dog. These eyes didn't look like that at all. A thick brow ran across them, making them look like those of a primate. Honestly, they resembled what Bigfoot's eyes might look like.

"No, it's a bear," I whispered again. "Gotta be."

Whatever the creature was, it was far away, and the shadows from the morning sun made it *look* more simian. That had to be it.

Not wanting to scare it away, I slowly reached into my pocket and pulled out my phone. Maybe if I got a photo, I could zoom in and prove to myself that it was only a bear.

Then I saw something that let me know it wasn't a bear at all. The creature had been so still that I hadn't noticed its arm before. But its long arm (much longer than a bear's) moved up as it released a small branch it had been holding down. The pair of eyes disappeared behind a clump of leaves.

I had been so mesmerized that I hadn't taken a picture. I finally pressed the button as an explosion of sound and movement happened twenty feet away. Whatever I saw had just disappeared over the slope of a small ravine.

I left the trail and gave chase. Running with a backpack is difficult, but running through dense vegetation with a backpack is nearly impossible. By the time I'd fought my way to the edge of the ravine, the creature was nowhere in sight. I remained perfectly still and scanned the woods. There was no movement, no sound, nothing. It was gone.

But *what* was gone?

THE EXPEDITION 4

JOE

I SCANNED THROUGH RADIO STATIONS AS FRANK and I drove home, desperate to fill the silence. My brother must have really been upset. Not only had he barely said two words all day, but it usually drives him crazy when I mess with his car stereo.

Finally I turned off the music. "Dude, it was just a prank."

"I know," Frank said. "Look, Benny apologized. Hector apologized. You apologized, and you were pranked along with me." He shook his head. "Just like I told Benny a hundred times, I'm over it. No big deal."

"Then why the silent treatment?" I asked.

"I just . . . ," Frank began. "I'm trying to figure something out."

"What?" I asked.

Frank tightened his lips. "On the way back down the trail, when I was alone, I saw . . . at least I *think* I saw—"

I slapped the dashboard so hard it made Frank jump. "Holy guacamole! You saw it, didn't you?!!"

"Hey!" Frank shouted. "Easy on the car."

"I can't believe it," I said. "The guy who doesn't believe in Bigfoot in the first place. The guy who thinks cryptozoology is bogus. The guy who—"

"Yeah, I get it," Frank cut me off.

"Dude, I'm so jealous." I settled into my seat. "What was it like?"

"First of all, I don't know exactly what I saw," he said. "Whatever it was, there has to be a logical explanation. That's what I'm trying to figure out."

I took in a deep breath. "Then let's work it out together. Tell me everything."

Frank related the story in detail. When he was done, I sat quietly, running through the facts in my mind.

Frank glanced over at me. "Thoughts?"

"You were quick to say it wasn't a bear," I said. "But what about another animal? A raccoon? A badger?"

Frank shook his head. "It was too big."

"A deer or elk?" I tried.

"Big, long, hairy arm, remember?" he said.

I thought for a second longer and then snapped my fingers. "Guy in a gorilla suit."

Frank tilted his head to the side. "I considered that, but

this thing moved fast. It took me forever to fight through all the undergrowth. Whatever this was zipped along as if it were nothing. No human could do that."

I shook my head. "I don't know, bro. Anything you're leaving out?"

"Just one." Frank dug into his pocket and pulled out his phone. "I got a picture."

I snatched the phone from his hand. "Don't you think you should've led with that?"

"Well . . . ," Frank began.

When I pulled up the photo, I realized why he hadn't. The image was one black blur surrounded by a green blur. The green part was so fuzzy that I could barely tell it was taken in the woods.

"Send this to CNN," I said sarcastically. "This is definitive proof."

"I know, right?" said Frank. "I'm packing a real camera next time."

I smiled. "Next time?"

"Look, I'm not saying I saw the Bayport Beast," said Frank. "But like you said, this is a mystery, and it's one I intend to solve."

"Whether you have the beast bug or not," I said, "count me in."

We went home to shower, wash our campfire-smoke-saturated clothes, and pack for a real expedition two days later. Frank made me promise not to tell our parents or our aunt Trudy about his sighting. As far as they were concerned, we were heading out on another backpacking trip, something we've done many times before.

"I can pack some food for you," Aunt Trudy offered.

"Thanks, Aunt T," I said. "But we're traveling light. We'll head over to Bayport Sports tomorrow and grab some packaged camp meals."

Aunt Trudy wrinkled her nose. "Dehydrated food. I don't see how anyone can call that a meal."

The next morning we set out on our supply run. We had two stops to make—the sporting goods store and Triple B Comics. Hopefully, Benny would make a copy of his map for us.

As we pulled up to the shop, Frank warned, "Not a word to Benny!"

"Seriously?" I asked. "Benny is one of the few people who would actually believe you."

Frank shook his head. "He'll want to come. We can cover more ground if we don't have to hear about every sighting in Bayport history."

I nodded. "True."

Frank sighed. "Plus . . . he'll never let me live it down."

I climbed out of the car. "Right on both counts, bro."

We entered the comic shop to find Benny at the front counter, hunched over a stack of paper. He looked up. "Hi, guys," he said. His eyes landed on my brother. "Look, Frank . . ."

My brother held up both hands. "Again, it's fine. No big deal."

I saw an opportunity. "You know how you can make it up to us?" I asked. "You can get us a copy of that map."

Benny's eyes lit up. "You're going back out?"

Frank shrugged. "Just for some hiking." He jutted a thumb in my direction. "Joe thought it would be cool to have a copy of your map."

I shook my head. My own brother had thrown me under the bus.

"Funny you should mention that." Benny reached toward the stack of pages he'd been studying when we walked in. "Check out my new product. Bayport Beast maps. Just ten bucks each."

Frank took one. "Aren't these the same trail maps they give out at the park's visitor center?"

"But I marked the location of every beast sighting," Benny said proudly.

Frank examined Benny's work. "You know that these maps are free at the park, right?"

Benny grinned. "Those don't have my marks."

"You're going to actually charge us after that stunt you pulled?" asked Frank in disbelief.

"Okay, I'll give you guys my friend rate—five bucks."

While my brother and Benny haggled over the price, I noticed that a man had entered the shop. He was tall and thin, and he wore a dark blue blazer and jeans. He had a bandage on his forehead, and his crazy brown hair looked as if it had been styled in the backseat of a convertible. The man scanned a few comic books on one of the big wall racks.

"Okay, okay, you can have one," Benny relented. "But if anyone asks, tell them where you got it. And that you paid full price."

I leaned in to get a closer look at the unfolded map. "And this is up to date?"

"That's the best part," Benny explained. "It's color coded. All the blue Xs are sightings from this year!"

Like Benny's map from our trip earlier, this one had large black Xs scattered around it. Three or four blue Xs were mixed in with the black ones in the main trail area, while on the right side of the map, far away from the other marked spots, was a cluster of blue Xs.

Frank eyed him suspiciously. "How do you know about all these sightings anyway? You never did tell us."

Benny glanced around the store, then leaned forward. "One of the park rangers gives me the inside scoop," he whispered.

"Isn't that against some confidentiality rule or something?" I asked.

Benny shook his head. "No, man. I just get the info a little before the public does."

I pointed to the blue Xs located away from the rest. "What about those?" I asked.

"Those sightings happened on the expert trails, and all

within the last week," Benny replied. "I would've taken us there, but it's almost a full day's hike, and they're steep."

I examined the trails leading to the cluster of marks. They were miles away from where Frank had had his sighting. I made a mental note to add my brother's sighting to the map later.

"So when are you guys heading out?" Benny asked.

"Well," Frank began, "we're not sure—"

"Excuse me," came a voice behind us. "May I purchase one of those maps?"

It was the guy with the wild hair.

"You bet," Benny replied.

"I saw your booth at the convention," the man told Benny. "And I thought I might have a moment of your time. You seem to be the resident expert on this Bayport Beast, setting up tours even."

Benny stood up a little straighter. "Well, I mean, I don't know if I'm an *expert*. . . ."

"Don't listen to him," I told the man. "He's the real deal."

"You see, I'm scouting locations for a TV show," the man continued. "You may have heard of it, *Stalking Sasquatch*?"

Benny grinned. "One of my favorites!" He turned to us. "These guys travel all over the country to investigate reported sightings, set up hidden cameras in the woods, and try to find definite proof of Bigfoot's existence."

It sounded exactly like every other Bigfoot reality show I had heard of, but if Benny the Beast liked it, then it must be one of the better ones.

Our excited friend spun back to the man. "I especially like Duncan Lane's Sasquatch call." Benny cupped his hands around his mouth, tilted his head back, and let out a series of short barks.

The man laughed. "I'll tell Duncan you're a fan." He held out a hand. "I'm Rex Johansson."

"Ben Williams," said Benny as he shook the man's hand.

I saw our perfect out. "Benny is your source for everything Bayport Beast." I nudged Frank as I backed away. "We'll leave you to it."

"Uh, yeah," Frank agreed. We were almost to the door. "Thanks for the map, Benny."

"Okay, guys," Benny said. "Text me when you go out to—" The door shut behind us, cutting off his sentence.

Frank and I jogged to the car. "That was close," I said.

5
THE BENEFACTOR

FRANK

GOTTA HAVE SPAGHETTI AND MEAT-balls," Joe said as he rattled a foil pouch. He dropped it into our cart with the others.

I counted about ten bags of dehydrated meals. "How long do you plan on camping out?"

Joe shrugged. "We have a mystery to solve, bro. No telling how long it'll take."

"You watch too many survival shows," I told him. "I'm not spending my entire summer chasing Bigfoot."

Shopping at Bayport Sports was always dangerous. They had the latest camping supplies, survival gear, and sporting equipment. If Joe wasn't threatening to spend his life's savings on a new catcher's mitt, I was busy drooling over the latest climbing harness.

"Hey, check these out!" Joe's voice came from the next aisle.

I pushed our cart over to the hunting section. This part of the store was chock-full of camouflage clothing, chemicals to mask human scent, and devices that imitated animal calls.

My brother was holding a clear package containing a box the size of a thick book. There were lenses on its front, and the entire thing was covered in a woodland camouflage pattern.

"Oh, a game camera! I've heard of those," I said. "Hunters strap them to trees to determine what kind of animals are in the area."

"Totally cheating," said Joe. "But check it out: it's motion activated *and* it has an infrared sensor." He pointed to a green-tinted photo of a deer on the back. "You leave it out overnight and then check the memory card in the morning to see what came by." He turned to me. "You thinking what I'm thinking?"

"I doubt it," I replied.

"A few of these would make our beast hunt so much easier," Joe explained. "Just like the guys in Benny's favorite Sasquatch show."

"You didn't check the price, as usual." I pointed to the rack of cameras. "The cheapest one here is way out of our price range."

Joe's shoulders sank. "I guess that's that."

"Perhaps I can help," said a voice behind us.

We both spun to see Rex Johansson standing there with a grin on his face.

"Hey, are you following us?" Joe asked half-jokingly.

Johansson's eyes widened. "No, no." He scratched his head. "Well, yes. I mean . . . your friend Ben said I might find you here. He suspects you are about to embark on a search for the Bayport Beast."

"Uh, we're just going camping," I said.

"Well, your friend also mentioned you've done some detective work in the past," he continued. "Seems that last year you lent your services to another production company while they filmed a movie here."

"That was us," Joe said proudly.

It was true that my brother and I had solved a case on the set of a cool zombie movie that was filming in Bayport. Someone was trying to sabotage the production, and we helped unmask the culprits. As usual, Police Chief Olaf wasn't so thrilled with our involvement. Of course, Olaf has never been happy with us working any case in Bayport. I think it has something to do with the fact that we make him look bad; we can usually solve cases a lot faster than he and his team can.

"Well, maybe you can help with my production," said Johansson. "We're very interested in this Bayport Beast of yours. And your friend Ben has been a wealth of information. We'll probably interview him for the show."

I smiled. "He's going to love that."

"How can we help?" Joe asked.

"I overheard you talking about these game cameras," Johansson explained. "I'd like to purchase a few and have you place them during your expedition." He gestured at the wall of cameras. "You can bring them back to me when you're finished."

"Why us?" I asked. "If you're here scouting locations, can't you place them?"

Johansson placed a hand on his chest. "I'm scouting locations in town, for interviews and whatnot." He glanced around. "To be completely honest, I detest camping."

Joe laughed. "Isn't that all the show is?" he asked. "A bunch of guys camping in the woods looking for Bigfoot?"

The man smiled. "Yes, but I'm not actually on the show. While our trackers are trudging around in the woods along with the mosquitos and bears, I'm in my nice clean hotel room."

"But what if the cameras don't photograph the beast?" I asked.

Johansson laughed. "Oh, I'm sure they won't. You watch the show, don't you? We never actually find proof of Bigfoot. It would be a short season if we did."

"So what good are the cameras?" I said.

"With this many sightings in one area, there's something out there," the man explained. "We always try to provide alternate theories during our show. Maybe it's someone in a gorilla suit, a rabid bear, a mange-ridden coyote . . . who knows? Hopefully you'll find out what it is."

Joe smiled at me. "Sounds like a mystery."

Johansson clapped his hands together. "Splendid!" He pulled five cameras off the rack and placed them in our cart.

We followed Mr. Johansson to the front of the store to check out. He offered to pay for our camp meals too, but I wouldn't let him. It didn't seem right, since we were going to buy them anyway.

Once outside, we loaded our borrowed gear into the car. Then Mr. Johansson spread out his copy of Benny's map. He pointed to the cluster of sightings on the main trail. "I want you to place the cameras around these sightings, here."

Joe pointed to the more recent cluster on the secluded trails. "What about over here?" he asked. "These happened not so long ago—last week, in fact."

The man shook his head. "Honestly, if our crew does come here, they won't be interested in those areas. Too remote and hard to reach." He reached into his pocket and pulled out a business card with a metallic silver logo that sparkled in the light. It looked like a tiny flagpole with a silver flag jutting out on each side. A spring circled the bottom of the pole, and the entire thing was enclosed within an upside-down silver triangle.

"Sorry, this is an old card." Johansson produced a pen and scratched out some information on the front of the card. When he was finished, all that was left were the logo and a phone number. He had written in his name. "Call me when you get back with the cameras."

MINOR ADJUSTMENT

6

JOE

"YOU'RE TOO SUSPICIOUS," I TOLD MY brother.

Frank typed Johansson's name into another search engine. "First that guy popped up at the convention, then the comic book shop, then the sporting goods store. He seems to turn up wherever we are. Of course I'm suspicious."

Ever since we'd returned home from the store, I'd been packing while Frank had been glued to his laptop. He'd searched *Stalking Sasquatch*'s official website as well as some other databases that listed cast and crew members, but so far he'd come up with nothing on Mr. Johansson.

"You know, if I have to pack your clothes for you too, you're not going to like it."

40

"I'm done, I'm done." Frank closed the laptop and hopped off the bed. He ran into his room to pack.

Luckily, most of our camping gear was still in our packs from the last trip; we just needed to stow food, plenty of water, and a couple of real cameras. Frank was finished minutes later.

"I couldn't find evidence of him anywhere," he admitted when he was back in my room. "I know not everyone has an obvious presence on the Internet, but I thought with him being in television there would be something."

"Think he works under a different name?" I asked. "It's been known to happen."

"Maybe," replied Frank. "But there's not a different name printed on the business card."

Frank had searched for the logo on the business card too. Unfortunately, my brother couldn't find anything on that, either. We'd assumed it was the logo for the show's production company, but it wasn't.

"And why did he scratch out that other info?" Frank asked, holding the business card up to the light. "I wonder if we could wash the ink off somehow."

"Dude, you're spending way too much time on this," I said.

I don't know why my brother was so interested in this guy. We had a real mystery on our hands (kinda), and someone asking us to solve it (also kinda). I know it wasn't the kind of mystery we usually solved, but I was thrilled that my brother was finally interested in cryptozoology.

But Frank's a Hardy, after all. Once you set us on a mystery, no matter how small, we're like bloodhounds; we don't stop until we find out where it ends. And hidden information, no matter how insignificant it may seem, is still a mystery.

I spread the map across my bed. Earlier that day, Frank had added his sighting to the map. I put a finger on the new mark. "I say we put a camera around here for sure."

Frank glanced at the map. "For sure."

I scanned the cluster of marks among the advanced trails. "I wonder why he doesn't want at least one camera up here. These sightings are way more current. It seems too good an opportunity to pass up."

"Maybe it's just like he said," Frank suggested. "Too hard to get to."

"Now who's taking him at face value?" I asked.

Frank smiled. "It was a good reason. Remember all the equipment the movie people used when they were here?"

I thought back to all the semitrailers parked along Cheshire Avenue. The production company had used big rigs to haul in the camera trailer, the makeup trailer, the special effects trailer, and more. The usually quiet residential street had resembled a crowded truck stop.

"I'm sure they don't use that much equipment for a reality show," Frank continued. "But even if they used a sixteenth of the gear, that's a lot to lug up those trails."

I scanned the map and traced my finger along a winding mountain road. "Yeah, they'd have to drive up Route 19." A bend in the road came close to a bend in one of the trails. "There's no way to safely park a big semi on that narrow road."

"Right," Frank agreed.

I leaned closer. "But you know what? We can."

Frank moved closer to the map. "What do you mean?"

"Check this out." I pointed to where the highway came closest to the trails. "We could park here and hike down to this trail here. It would be a lot faster than hiking through the main trailhead."

Frank shook his head. "I'm not leaving my car overnight on a blind curve."

"I'm not talking overnight," I explained. "What if we park there just long enough to place one of the cameras on those trails?"

Frank scratched the back of his head. "Not a bad idea. Though Mr. Johansson did tell us to forget about those sightings."

I nodded. "Yeah, but this is still our investigation, right? I know you want to check out the place where you had your sighting. Getting footage of these fresh ones seems like a no-brainer."

Frank raised an eyebrow. "Well, he did say he didn't expect us to find anything."

I smiled. "It's a plan then."

SIGNS OF LIFE

7

FRANK

THE NEXT MORNING WE LOADED OUR gear into my car, and I drove us up to the blind curve Joe had pointed out the previous day. It took Joe navigating several mountain roads and heavy reliance on the GPS on his phone, but we finally made it.

"This is it!" Joe announced.

"I was afraid you were going to say that," I said.

The two-lane road was cut into the side of the mountain. I pulled to the right and onto the narrow shoulder. To our left, the landscape dropped off into the national forest below. Luckily, there didn't seem to be anyone else traveling the road.

We climbed out of the car. Fresh skid marks on the

pavement reminded me that this wasn't the safest place to leave my car. I pointed them out to Joe. "Let's make this quick," I said. "Looks like someone already wiped out here."

Joe threw a leg over the low guardrail. "No kidding." He knocked on the shiny metal. "This section looks like it was recently replaced."

My brother and I can't help but see clues wherever we go. Evidence of a past accident couldn't have been more apparent if we had read about it in the paper. When we gazed over the side, we saw snapped and splintered trees pointing down the mountainside. The crashed vehicle had been removed, but its path of destruction was still there.

"Whoa," Joe whispered.

The accident did make our trip down the steep incline a bit easier; there was no thick underbrush to climb over. My brother and I moved down the cleared path with relative ease.

Once we made it to the crash site, I forged ahead through the woods. I wasn't ten feet in before it opened up onto a hiking trail.

"That was easy," Joe said. He took off his pack and dug inside for a game camera.

I pulled out the map and marched to part of the trail that marked one of the sightings. I pointed to a tall tree just off the trail. "How about there? We could aim it back at the trail."

"Shouldn't we choose a less conspicuous game trail or something?" Joe asked. "Wouldn't the beast want to stay away from people?"

I shrugged. "Here's the way I see it: if any animal was spotted here, it will probably be back. Creatures of habit and all that."

"True," Joe agreed. "And an animal that large would make use of the big trails anyway, especially these secluded ones."

"Exactly. And if it's just some guy in a suit, he'd stay on the main trails too."

"Another good point," said Joe.

I glanced back up the way we had come. "Besides, I don't want to leave my car up on that blind curve while we search for just the right game trail."

Joe strapped the camera to a tree and stepped back. "What do you think?"

It took a second for me to spot the device. Its camouflage casing made it blend seamlessly into the bark and surrounding foliage.

"Perfect," I replied. "Let's get back."

Climbing back up to the road took about twice as long, but we made it without incident. My car was right where I'd left it (not rear-ended by a speed demon) and we climbed in.

"One down, four to go," Joe said.

I drove back to the national forest visitor center. After I parked and we unloaded our gear, we consulted the map once more. The night before, we had circled all the locations where we wanted to place cameras. The second stop on our list was near where I'd had my sighting.

My phone buzzed in my pocket. "A text from Benny. He wants to know when we're heading out."

Joe shrugged. "Ignore?"

"That's rude," I replied.

"We're on a case," Joe explained. "Completely justified."

I nodded and returned the phone to my pocket. Benny would have to wait.

Joe and I started up the main trail. We passed several hikers along the way, both coming up and going down. Even though traffic on the path wasn't too heavy, we'd have to be careful to make sure nobody saw us place the cameras. The last thing we needed was someone swiping one of them.

It didn't take us long to reach our first spot in this area, the place where I had seen . . . whatever I saw.

Joe spun around so that his back was to me. "You place this one and I'll keep a lookout."

I pulled the camera out of my brother's pack and he quickly hiked farther up the trail. He positioned himself on a rise so he could look out for any hikers approaching from either direction. I stepped a few feet into the woods, away from where I had seen the creature. I wanted to make sure the camera caught not only the spot where the thing had been hiding but also the trail itself. After checking the angle one last time, I strapped it to a tree and switched it on.

Before returning to the trail, I scanned the woods, but the thick underbrush and dark shadows hid most of the sloping terrain. There were so many places to hide. The Bayport

Beast could be out there watching us and we wouldn't even know. I listened for any signs of movement but heard only birdsong, the breeze whistling through the treetops, and the distant drumming of a woodpecker.

No sooner had I stepped back onto the trail when I heard two short whistles—a signal from my brother that someone was coming. I made a show of checking the straps on my pack as a family of four hiked past. I nodded a greeting and then hiked up to join my brother.

"Done," I told him.

We spent the rest of the day setting up the cameras. There were only three left, but we wanted to space them as far apart as possible. We took our time, keeping an eye out for the Bayport Beast (or whatever it was I saw that day).

"They could be aliens," Joe said as we hiked.

"What could be aliens?" I asked.

"You know, the Bigfoots," he replied.

I sighed. "How do you figure that they're aliens?"

"Maybe they were sent here to observe us," he explained. "But they're too big and hairy to blend into human society. So they have to live in the woods."

"What could they observe about us while they hang out in the forest?" I asked. "The latest style of hiking boot?"

Joe laughed. "I didn't say it was a good theory. But it is a theory."

"Barely," I said.

Once the last game camera had been strapped into place,

we made our way deeper into the woods to set up camp. We found an open space off the main trail, and I assembled the tent while Joe built a campfire. Before long, we were digging into the hot foil packages of our rehydrated dinner.

"I'm starving," Joe said in between steaming mouthfuls of noodles.

I was halfway through my meal when my phone buzzed for the twentieth time that day. I didn't have to look to know who it was. "Benny again," I said between bites.

Both Joe and I had received texts from our friend all day long. We'd had reprieves in the valleys or thicker parts of the forest where there was no cell reception. However, as soon as we crested a hill, both of our phones had buzzed with missed texts from Benny.

"He's not taking a hint, is he?" Joe asked.

"I'm starting to feel really bad now," I said. "I'm not even reading them anymore."

"How about this?" Joe suggested. "We'll text him back tomorrow and tell him we're on our way home. Tell him there was spotty cell reception in the forest."

I held up my fork. "At least part of that is true."

Joe wolfed down the last bit of his dinner. "Let's get some more hiking in while there's plenty of light," he suggested.

"Good idea," I agreed. "We can hit some of the other sighting locations."

We packed away our trash and grabbed our cameras. Without heavy backpacks, we made better time through the narrow trails. I enjoyed the hike, but we didn't spot anything.

"Maybe it's the beast's day off," Joe suggested.

We topped another rise and saw that the trail divided below us. I checked the map. "These trails meet again on the next hill," I said. "Want to split up?"

"Sure thing," Joe replied. "Never a bad move in a horror movie."

I laughed. "Good thing this isn't a horror movie."

I veered right as my brother disappeared behind the foliage to my left. I kept a steady pace, stopping only to take a photo of a small woodpecker on a nearby tree. After it flew away, the woods were silent around me.

After such an uneventful day, I began to question my earlier sighting. It had seemed so real at the time, but maybe I had been imagining things. Like most memories, the image in my mind seemed to grow fuzzy with the passage of time. Maybe it *had* been just a bear.

I pushed away all thoughts of Sasquatch and took in a deep breath, smiling as the earthy air filled my lungs. I loved being out in nature, away from civilization and the sights, sounds, and smells that came with it. Here it was just me, the tweeting of distant birds, and the steady rhythm of my hiking boots crunching along the trail.

The path ahead dipped across a dry creek, then jutted up another hill and disappeared to the left. As I hiked down to the creek, I saw I wouldn't have to worry about mud on my hiking boots. The soil was merely soft from a rainstorm—not slippery or muddy.

However, just before I stepped into the dry bed, I spotted something that froze me in my tracks.

There was a footprint in the soft earth—a very big footprint. It had the shape of a human foot, but it was close to two feet long.

It couldn't be a Bigfoot footprint . . . could it?

SIGHTING 8

JOE

DID I ACTUALLY THINK WE WOULD SPOT the Bayport Beast? I don't know. But if we did, I was ready. My camera was clutched in both hands as I moved briskly down the trails.

After Frank and I had split up, I figured I would cover more ground than him. Keeping my eyes open for anything strange, my competitive side kicked in. I knew I could beat him to the place where the trails rejoined.

The path dipped and crossed an old creek. I hopped over the dry creek bed and was getting ready to lean into the climb ahead when I heard a rustle in the woods to my right. I slowed to a stop and scanned the woods: nothing but trees, trees, and more trees. The undergrowth was thick, but I didn't think a full-grown Sasquatch would hide so close to the trail.

I waited and listened a bit longer. Nothing. I turned and began climbing up the steep trail.

There was another rustle and what sounded like a twig snapping. I halted again, but all I heard were chirping birds. Then another snap. I slowly turned and searched the woods again. Nothing.

Movement caught the corner of my eye. I widened my view to include the spot where the trail crossed the creek bed.

A dark shape lumbered past thick tree trunks and behind leafy undergrowth. Branches swung and more twigs snapped as whatever it was crept closer to the trail. The dark form shrank momentarily as if ducking under a branch before moving closer. Then the thing emerged from behind the last tree and stood in the center of the dry creek bed. Out of the woods, unobstructed, there it was— the Bayport Beast!

I felt two conflicting emotions: elation that I was actually looking at a mythical figure, and pure fear. Even though I was partway up the next hill, this thing was massive: at least seven feet tall. It was covered with matted brown hair, and its two dark eyes seemed to bore into me.

The detective in me was ready to gather evidence, but my primal self was ready to drop the camera and get out of there.

Luckily, the detective part won out as I slowly raised the camera to my face. Either the creature wasn't a fan of paparazzi or my movement spooked it. Whatever it was, the beast turned and thundered back into the woods. I barely got a shot off before it disappeared down the dry creek bed.

I ran down the hill, trying to get another shot, before realizing that it was heading straight for my brother. I had to warn him!

I dug out my phone and checked the coverage—only one bar. I hoped the signal would hold as I shot Frank a quick text.

After I sent the text, I almost pursued the creature into the woods. Almost. Now my primal half took over. I didn't want to corner that thing between my brother and me. Instead, I ran up the hiking trail. Hopefully, I could reach the split and then double back to my brother's trail.

I just hoped Frank could hold it together until then.

NO JOKE 9

FRANK

TOOK A STEP BACK AND SNAPPED WHAT seemed like my hundredth photo of the footprint. I didn't know if it was real or some kind of joke. The impression had five toes and was shaped exactly like a human footprint—only twice as large. It looked as if Shaquille O'Neal's big brother had hiked through.

I smiled. Joe was going to be so jealous that he didn't find it first.

My phone vibrated; probably another text from Benny. I almost ignored it, but I felt too guilty. I pulled out my phone to find a single text from Joe.

BEAST COMING YOUR WAY! DOWN CREEK BED. LOOK OUT!!!

I shook my head. Enough with the pranks! I was about to reply when a sound distracted me—something moving along the creek to my left. The sound of rustling branches grew louder. Was Joe serious?

I dashed down the trail, back the way I had come. When I was about fifteen feet away from the creek, I slid behind the trunk of a tree just off the path. I crouched down and aimed my camera at the creek and focused the telephoto lens.

A massive creature plodded into frame and I pressed the shutter release. My camera clicked away as I captured frame after frame what looked like the Bayport Beast! The thing was huge and hairy, with a mix of human and simian facial features. It looked exactly like every description of Bigfoot I'd read or heard about.

The beast swung its head from side to side as if making sure no one was on its trail. Its movements were puzzling. It leaned forward and put its hands on its knees, just like a human trying to catch their breath. The beast's fur-covered chest rose and fell as it panted.

I slowly got to my feet. This thing was acting *very* human.

The beast glanced over its shoulder at the creek behind it before reaching a hand to its neck. It tugged on the fur, seeming to stretch its skin. I cringed. As it pulled its skin farther and farther out from its body, it became clear: this was a mask. Sure enough, the "beast" was just a person in a suit!

The imposter's back was to me, so I couldn't get any facial features. I took a couple more photos before stepping out onto the trail. "Hey!" I shouted.

The person fumbled with the mask, pulling it back down over his or her head before glancing back to find me standing in the middle of the trail.

The "beast" took off, running up the trail in long, loping strides. I had to pour on the speed to keep up. Luckily, the uphill trail slowed the imposter down.

The counterfeit beast skidded to a stop as Joe came into view. My brother froze, not ten feet away from the creature, his eyes wide with shock.

"It's okay," I said as I jogged up the hill. "It's someone in a suit."

Joe leaned forward and squinted. "No kidding." He stepped closer.

The phony giant shot looks at me, Joe, and then back at me. It turned as if it were going to make a break for it.

"Don't even think about it," I warned.

I didn't know what I would do if the imposter tried to run. Whoever was wearing the suit was huge. One thing was for sure: without our heavy backpacks, Joe and I could make our way through the thick forest much faster. We might not be able to hold him, but we wouldn't lose him.

The beast turned back to Joe, raised its arms, and took a giant step forward as if it were about to attack.

Joe crossed his arms and shook his head. "Not buying it!"

The beast rounded on me. I didn't back down either. Instead, I raised my camera and snapped a few more pics. "Smile."

The creature's shoulders sank. Two hairy hands reached up and pulled off the mask to reveal a familiar face.

"Benny?!!" Joe shouted.

I looked him up and down. "You grew!"

ANOTHER MINOR ADJUSTMENT

10

JOE

I WENT FROM SOARING EXCITEMENT (OKAY, with some fear mixed in) to crushing disappointment in a matter of seconds as I hiked down to join my brother and the surreal Sasquatch. It was as if our friend's head had been plopped on top of a Bigfoot body. Even brown face paint surrounded his eyes—no doubt to keep his pale skin from showing through the mask's eyeholes.

"Hi, guys," he said with a nervous laugh. "How's it going?"

"How's it going?" I repeated, throwing up my arms. "We just found our friend running around pretending to be Bigfoot."

"So that's why you've been texting us all day?" Frank asked. "You wanted to find out where we'd be so you could prank us again?"

"Not cool, dude," I added.

Benny shook his head. "It's not like that. I really wanted to go camping with you guys. You know, to look for the beast."

"Wait a minute." I crossed my arms. "You wanted to look for the Bayport Beast, dressed as the beast?"

Benny waved me away. "No, man. When you guys didn't text back, I just came out here to do my own thing. It's such a big park that I didn't expect to run into you."

"And your *thing* is dressing up as the Bayport Beast?" I said.

Benny shrugged. "Well . . . yeah."

"So you've been the Bayport Beast this entire time?" Frank questioned him.

"Of course not," Benny replied. "I only started doing it this year to drum up interest, you know?"

"And drive up sales of your new beast merch," Frank added.

Our friend smiled sheepishly. "Well, it didn't hurt."

"Benny." I sighed. I was torn. Our friend had not only tricked us into believing he was the Bayport Beast; he had essentially betrayed the trust of a fellow beast hunter, namely me. But his costume *was* pretty cool, and I had to admit that I was impressed. "So what is that?" I asked him. "A gorilla costume?"

Benny looked down at his arms. "Mostly. Then I added matching fur to a Cro-Magnon man mask."

He handed me the mask for a closer look. Benny had done a pretty good job adding extra hair and painting the skin.

I pointed to Benny's long legs. "What about your new-found height?"

"These are drywall stilts." Benny bent over and tugged at one of his furry legs. The bottom of the costume rose to reveal two metal poles where his ankles should have been. They disappeared into a fake Bigfoot foot. "People walk around on these when they install drywall on ceilings. My cousin works in construction, and he gave me his old pair."

"And the feet?" Frank asked.

"Plywood and more fake fur," Benny revealed proudly. "I cut them into the shapes of real feet so I could leave a big footprint."

Frank gestured to the creek bed behind him. "Yeah, I saw one of those. Got a ton of pictures of a genuine *fake* Bigfoot footprint."

"Pretty realistic, huh?" Benny asked.

I shook my head. "Well, I guess that's it. Mystery solved." I tossed the mask back to Benny. "Let's round up the cameras and take them back to Mr. Johansson."

"Mr. Johansson?" Benny asked.

Frank and I explained how Johansson had asked us to place cameras around the trails.

"Some of them probably caught footage of you in your Bigfoot suit," I added. "We're going to have to tell him about this."

Benny waved his furry hands. "Aw, you can't do that. He was going to use me in the show."

"How can you be on the show as a Bayport Beast expert when you *are* the beast?" I asked.

"But I'm not," Benny pleaded. "I was just messing around." He glanced from Frank to me. "There really is a Bayport Beast. I can prove it."

I laughed. "Yeah, right." I nudged my brother's arm. "Can you believe this guy?"

Frank held up a hand. "Let's hear him out."

"Wait, so you're the believer now?" I asked my brother. "You're the guy who thought this was all bogus to begin with."

"Yeah, but I'm also the guy who saw . . . whatever it is I saw," Frank said. "And Benny was with you at the time, remember? He has an alibi."

My mouth dropped open. "Oh, man. You're right."

Benny's eyes went from Frank to me and then back to Frank. "What are you talking about?"

Frank retold the story of his encounter with the Bayport Beast. It sounded just as creepy the second time around.

"You saw the beast and didn't tell me?" Benny asked.

"Really?" I asked him. "You *were* the beast and didn't tell us!"

Benny ignored the accusation. "That just proves my point. There is something out here."

Frank thought for a moment. "Maybe we should spend the night and see what the cameras find after all."

"Can I stay with you guys? Please?" Benny pleaded.

"Only if you promise to wash your face first," I said. "You look like a raccoon."

We followed Benny back to his campsite, and he changed out of his beast costume. We helped him strike his tent and pack his gear. Soon Benny was back to his normal height and carrying the oversize backpack that held his beast costume along with his camping gear.

We made it back to our campsite before dark. As we sat around the fire, Frank unfolded the map and showed Benny where we had placed the cameras.

"Those are good spots," said Benny.

"Yeah, but how many of those more recent sightings on the main trails were you?" asked Frank.

Benny winced. "All of them but yours."

"Benny!" Frank barked.

Benny shrugged. "Sorry."

I pointed to the secluded trails. "Don't forget the camera up here." I shot Benny a look. "I guess that was you too."

Benny shook his head. "No way. I never made it all the way up to those trails."

Frank and I exchanged a look. I tapped the map again. "So none of the most recent sightings there were you?"

"No." He raised a hand, palm out. "I swear. According to my inside source, all of those happened last week. I was hoping to check them out soon, but . . ." He grinned sheepishly. "I was having too much fun playing the beast myself."

I stared at my brother. "You know, that camera is probably the only one *without* a photo of Benny the Beast on its memory card."

Frank nodded. "It's a long hike."

"How fast can we round up the other cameras tomorrow?" I asked.

Frank pursed his lips. "If we leave our gear here, split up, grab the cameras, and pick up our packs on the way out . . ."

"What are you guys talking about?" Benny asked.

"I hope your pack's not too heavy." I said as I clamped a hand on Benny's shoulder. "Because if you're sticking with us, you're going to get plenty of exercise tomorrow."

We went to sleep early so we could rise at first light. The next morning, after a quick breakfast—rehydrated huevos rancheros—we struck camp, hid our backpacks, and jogged down to retrieve the cameras we had placed the day before.

My brother and I had come to the same conclusion. If we were going to truly solve this mystery, the advanced trails were the place to be. There was something going on up there that didn't involve our friend in a gorilla suit.

After picking up all the cameras on the main trail, we met up back at the campsite in just over an hour. We pulled on our packs and began our long trek to the more secluded part of the trail system.

It was going to take most of the day to get there before dark. This time Benny didn't slow us down like we had originally feared. Maybe it was his heavy backpack or our quick pace or the fact that he had been busted as a phony Bigfoot. Whatever it was, he didn't tell a single beast story along the way.

Benny got a text about an hour after lunch. "There's been another sighting," he announced.

We stopped and I dug the map out of Frank's pack. "Where?"

Benny pointed to a spot on the map just off one of the secluded trails. "Right here. I'll add it to the small cluster of *X*s."

I folded the map. "I wonder what your park ranger will think when she finds out you were behind of a lot of the sightings."

"Don't forget about Mr. Johansson," Frank added.

"Ah, come on, guys," Benny pleaded.

For the rest of the hike, he begged us not to tell anyone about him wearing the Bigfoot suit.

His tactic worked, though. By the end of the day, Frank and I were worn down.

"Fine," I said. "We won't tell anyone about your forest costume party."

"If you promise not to do it again," Frank added.

Benny nodded frantically. "I promise! I promise!"

The sun sank lower and lower in the sky as we made our way to the outer trails. Once we were there, we consulted the map to find our way to the crash site. Benny's eyes widened when he saw the path of snapped trees and plowed earth leading back up to the highway. "Whoa, you weren't kidding," he said. "This accident must've been a doozy."

We hunted for the game camera, hoping it had picked up something from the night before.

Frank pointed to a bare tree trunk. "I thought it was right here."

"You must have your trees mixed up, bro," I said, glancing around.

We split up and checked the nearby trees. Even though the camera was camouflaged, Frank and I knew what it looked like. It shouldn't have been that hard to spot.

"Uh, guys?" asked Benny. He held up a mangled plastic box. "Is this it?"

"Oh, man," I muttered as Frank and I jogged over to Benny.

The plastic casing had been pried open, and circuit boards dangled from frayed wires.

"Did a bear get it?" asked Benny.

"Maybe vandals," I suggested, turning the mangled plastic in my hands. "I don't see any teeth marks."

Frank dug around in the camera's disemboweled circuitry. "We'll find out soon enough." He pulled out a small square. "That is, if the memory card is still readable."

Frank replaced his camera's memory card with the one from the game camera. We gathered around the small screen as my brother scanned through the images. As we suspected, there were shots of different hikers frozen mid-stride. When he came to the night-vision photos, all of the images had a green tint to them. There were shots of a raccoon and a coyote, and two separate photos of deer. Each of the animals had glowing eyes from the infrared light on the camera. Frank stopped on the last frame.

"Oh, man," Benny said.

"Is that . . . ," I began.

"Exactly what I saw the other day," Frank finished.

A huge, hairy hand covered most of the frame, as if its owner had been reaching for the lens. The background showed part of the creature's face: an angry low brow atop two glowing eyes.

THE BEAST LIVES

LIVES

11

FRANK

WHEN I WAS SURE THE LAST CAMERA was secure, I switched it on and made my way back to the trail. I banged my shin on a log and chided myself for not turning on my flashlight. It wasn't dark yet, but the sun had already dipped below the tree line. Whenever I'm camping, I try to use a flashlight as little as possible. It's better to let my eyes adjust to the ambient light (especially moonlight) and not blind myself or my friends with a flashlight's harsh beam. Unfortunately, there wasn't any moonlight yet, and the way back to the trail was thick with obstacles.

I stepped onto the clear trail and gazed back at the game camera. My eyes had adjusted just enough to glimpse a small reflection off the camera's lens. It had a clear view of the trail.

The three of us had decided to split up and place the rest of the cameras before dark. Even though we were all a little spooked from the photo, we figured splitting up would be the quickest way to get the job done.

As I rounded a bend toward our new campsite, I spotted two flashlight beams bobbing along the trail ahead. For a moment, I thought Joe and Benny had come looking for me. Then I spotted two more sweeping beams behind them.

The beams drew nearer, and I squinted as one shone right in my face.

"Whoops, sorry!" said a woman's voice. She lowered the flashlight.

Two couples who looked like they were in their twenties stood on the trail before me.

"That's all right," I said. "I didn't think anyone else was camping up here."

"I think we're it," said the other woman. "You're the only other person we've seen in two days."

"You camped here last night?" I asked.

"Yeah," said the first woman. She pointed to the trail behind me. "We're just over that hill."

"Did you see anything . . . weird last night?" I asked.

The group exchanged glances. "No. Why?"

"Just curious," I said (which was the truth, really). "It's my first night this deep in the trails."

"You'll love it," said the first woman. "Very quiet."

"Except for last night," one of the men corrected. "I think someone was hunting way out there in the woods. I thought I heard a gunshot."

"You all alone out here?" asked the other man.

I shook my head and pointed past them. "I'm camping with some friends over there."

"Well, have fun," said the first man as they made their way past me.

I watched them go, their flashlights scanning the trail before them. Good thing I had placed the camera before they arrived. I don't know how I would have explained that one.

When I returned to the campsite, Joe and Benny were already sitting in front of a roaring campfire. There was a pot of water over the flames.

"There he is," said Joe. "I thought the beast had you!" He was joking, of course, but I spotted a glimmer of relief on his face.

I told them about the other campers on the hill and their report about the gunshot from the night before.

"You're not supposed to hunt in this forest," Benny remarked.

"People aren't supposed to run around impersonating Bigfoot, either," said Joe.

I plopped down in front of the fire. "Are all the cameras in place?"

Joe held up a thumb. "Good to go."

Benny's eyes lit up. "We're bound to get some awesome shots off one of them."

"Unless the beast decides to trash them, too," muttered Joe. "I don't think Mr. Johansson's going to like that."

"Are you kidding?" I asked. "He'll probably get more cool shots like the other one."

"Let's see it again!" Benny demanded.

I dug out my camera while Joe dug out our dinner. Benny peered over my shoulder as I pulled up the image.

"You think it's a guy in a suit, like me?" asked Benny.

"I don't know," I replied. "Not much of its face is showing."

"A bear?" Joe asked.

"I can't say for sure on that, either," I admitted. "The game camera wasn't clawed or chewed." I zoomed in on the image. "And since whatever it was is so close to the lens, I can't be sure if that's a hand or a paw."

I put the camera away and we ate dinner silently and quickly. I don't know if we were that hungry or if we only wanted to get to sleep. Maybe both. It had been a long day of constant hiking up and down rugged terrain. If the others felt anything like me, they'd be asleep before the tent was zipped shut.

We said our good nights and climbed into our tents. Even though I was excited by what the game cameras would reveal, sleep came easily. My body was exhausted. I quickly drifted off to the relaxing sound of crickets chirping and the wind rustling through the trees.

A loud growl ripped me from my sleep. I sprang up, my hand on my flashlight, eyes darting around the tent. But it was only my brother's snoring.

I yawned as I pulled on my boots and climbed out of the tent. The full moon bathed the forest floor in silver light. I didn't even need my flashlight as I shuffled deeper into the trees to answer my own call of nature.

I returned to the tent, enjoying the feeling of cool air on my skin. I glanced at Benny's tent and noticed that his big backpack was lying on the ground in front of it. But something looked strange. When I took a closer look at the backpack, I realized it was flatter than it should have been, especially with the Bigfoot costume inside. I poked the fabric, which deflated under my touch. It was empty.

My lips tightened in anger. Benny better not have put on the costume. I couldn't believe he'd have the nerve to pull this prank again. I switched on my flashlight and shined it through the netting in the front of Benny's tent. Benny was gone. Joe and I should have confiscated his Bigfoot suit!

The other campers had said they were over the nearest hill, so I tried to walk in that direction, figuring that Benny had intended to scare them. The undergrowth was thin around our campsite, so I decided to forgo the trail and cut through the woods.

After traveling for about five minutes, I spotted Benny

in full costume, squatting on the forest floor. His back was to me, so he didn't see me approach. As I moved closer, I noticed he was crouching over something or someone on the ground. I couldn't make out what it was, so I readied my flashlight as I moved forward.

"Benny," I whispered. "What are you doing?"

When he heard my voice, Benny's shoulders stiffened and he growled.

"Cut the nonsense," I said. "You're so busted!"

Then I caught a glimpse of what Benny was huddled over. At first I didn't believe it. Then I switched on my flashlight and saw it clearly: a small, hairless . . . Bigfoot?

The crouching figure that I thought was Benny spun so fast that I stumbled back and dropped my flashlight. It took a giant step toward me.

ROOOOOAR!

Rows of sharp teeth gleamed in the moonlight. This definitely wasn't Benny. It was a Bigfoot.

The Bayport Beast was real?!

I tried to turn around, but I stumbled again and thudded into something behind me. Another, shorter Bigfoot glared up at me. It grabbed my arm with long, bony fingers. I was surrounded.

Terror took over. I broke free from the creature's grasp and dashed out from between the two beasts. Unfortunately, terror isn't a good navigator. In my haste, I slammed into a tree trunk.

You know how cartoon characters always see stars when they get hit in the head? That really happens—sort of. When my head hit the hard bark, a million pinpricks of light filled my vision. Before I knew it, my back hit the ground. As I stared up at the treetops, two looming figures filled my vision. The moonlight silhouetted their hairy forms and glinted off their piercing eyes. The last thing I saw was a massive pair of hands grabbing me. Then everything turned black.

TRAPPED 12

JOE

A DISTANT ROAR WOKE ME FROM A deep sleep. I rolled over and noticed that Frank's sleeping bag was empty.

I climbed out of the tent and scanned the area but didn't see my brother. "Frank?" I whispered. "Frank!" There was no answer.

It could have been the way I woke up, but I had a bad feeling about my brother. I grabbed my flashlight and tiptoed over to Benny's tent. When I peered through the screen opening, it was empty. I also spotted his empty backpack lying on the ground.

"Benny, really?" I said. "You couldn't even make it twenty-four hours without pranking?"

I shined my light into the surrounding woods. "Benny? Frank?" No answer.

I had no idea where Frank had gone, but I had a good idea where Benny was. I cut through the woods toward the other campers' campsite. I had a feeling my brother would've made the same deduction. Hopefully, if I found one I would find the other.

I moved quickly through the forest, my flashlight beam sweeping the area around me. Then I spotted a tiny shaft of light ahead. As I came closer, I saw that it was coming from the ground. When I was right on top of it, I reached down and picked up a flashlight. It was the same mini LED flashlight as the one in my hand. Frank's flashlight.

Not good.

I swept my flashlight around. "Frank!" I shouted. There was no sign of him.

My brother was the true outdoorsman of the family. He was certainly more at home in the forest than me. He didn't even use a flashlight most of the time. Needless to say, if I was missing and Frank was the one searching, he might've been able to pick up my trail on the forest floor. I didn't pretend to be as skilled, but I had to try.

I trained my light on the ground where I had found Frank's flashlight. Clumps of dirt and pine needles were strewn about, so I could tell something had happened there. A struggle, maybe?

Then I saw something that made me catch my breath—a

dark pool of liquid. It glistened bright red under my flashlight's beam. Blood.

I had to keep going toward the other campers. I couldn't pick up Frank's trail, but that was definitely where he had been heading. If I tried for any other direction, I could be wandering out there all night—maybe getting lost myself.

When I got to the base of the hill, I caught another flash of light in the woods to my left. I killed my flashlight and let my eyes adjust to the darkness. A warm glow seeped through the trees.

I slowly moved toward the glow with just the moonlight guiding me. Upon closer inspection, I saw it came from a camp lantern. Had I already made it to the other campsite? Maybe Frank had heard it wrong and they were on this side of the hill.

I crept closer to the campsite, all the while expecting to hear voices, laughter, maybe even singing: the usual things one hears around a campfire. But the campsite was silent.

I skirted around a clump of trees and snuck in for a closer look. The campsite appeared to be empty. There was a small one-man tent in the center of the lantern light, which didn't sound like the group Frank had described. I hated to disturb a random camper, but my brother was missing, and that was a lot of blood back there.

I stepped out from behind a tree. "Hello? Anyone home?" There was no answer, so I moved into the light. "Hello?"

The open tent flap fluttered in the cool breeze. I peeked

in; there was no one inside. The entire camp had a strange setup, including a small folding chair and table with what looked like a radio sitting on top. It almost looked like a shortwave receiver. A pick and a shovel were lying on the ground beside the tent. Was somebody prospecting for gold out here?

GRRRRR!

An ear-shattering growl sounded from the forest. Instinctively, I ducked down beside the camp table. Whatever that was sounded big and frustrated.

GRRR! GRR! GRR! GRR!

It didn't seem to be getting closer. I couldn't tell what kind of animal noise it was, so I did what any idiot alone in the woods would do; I decided to investigate.

I crept into the thick trees, pausing to let my eyes readjust to the moonlight before gingerly moving around the foliage. Keeping my flashlight at the ready, I navigated by moonlight alone. I kept a snail's pace so I wouldn't trip over a branch or snap a twig—anything to alert the beast to my whereabouts.

The forest opened up into a small clearing. The dim moonlight revealed a dark shape inside the ring of trees; a figure that appeared to be hunched over. It grunted as it rocked back and forth, almost as if it was struggling with something on the ground. As I slunk forward, the thing seemed to get more agitated.

"Ugh! Let go!" grunted a familiar voice.

I lit up the beast with my flashlight. "Benny!"

An overly hairy Cro-Magnon face turned toward me. "Joe!" Benny said from under the mask. "Help me out, man!"

I stepped around Benny and aimed my light at the ground. One of his ankles was caught in the jagged jaws of a bear trap. The trap was chained to a spike in the ground. I hissed when I saw how close the teeth were to touching each other. It looked as if my friend's ankle had been crushed.

Benny waved a hand when he saw my pained expression. "It's okay. It's stuck on the stilt, not my leg."

"Can't you take off the stilts?" I asked.

"Yeah, but I'll have to rip the suit to do it," he replied. "I don't want to do that!"

I wanted to remind Benny that he wasn't supposed to be wearing the suit in the first place. Instead I asked, "Have you seen Frank?"

Benny gave me puzzled look. "No, why?"

"He's missing," I said. I didn't bring up the pool of blood yet. One catastrophe at a time.

"Get me out of here and we'll find him," said Benny.

I knelt and grabbed one half of the bear trap with both hands. Benny took the other side and we pulled against each other. We grunted with effort, but the jaws barely moved.

Benny glanced around. "Find a big branch or something we can use to pry this open."

"We don't have time," I said. "Rip the suit."

"Come on, man," Benny pleaded. "Just try to find something."

I sighed as I ran to the edge of the clearing. We didn't have time for this. I frantically swept my light across the forest floor, looking for a stick or a branch beefy enough to work on that trap, but everything I saw was light and rotting.

"This is stupid," I murmured. "He's ripping the suit and we're finding Frank."

I jogged back toward the clearing and was almost there when I saw movement to my right. A man entered the clearing just before me. Benny's back was to the man, so he didn't see the stranger. The man halted and raised a rifle to his shoulder. He aimed the weapon at Benny's back.

"Hey!" I shouted. "Stop!"

The man ignored me and kept the rifle trained on Benny.

I bolted toward the man, my heart thumping in my chest. I was about twenty feet away as the stranger settled his cheek against the stock. I was ten feet away when the man put his finger on the trigger.

I wasn't going to make it.

MORE SIGNS

13

FRANK

BANG!

My eyes snapped open at the sound of a distant gunshot. I immediately slammed them tight again as the pain in my forehead flared, consuming my thoughts. I reached up and touched a spot above my eyes. When I drew my hand back, a dollop of blood glistened on my fingertips.

I lay there for a moment to let the world's biggest headache subside a bit. I would have waited longer if something hadn't stirred beside me. I turned my head and saw the Bayport Beast sitting on the ground beside me.

Startled, I jumped and began to scramble away. That set my headache straight to the moon. A wave of nausea stopped me cold, and I couldn't do anything but sit back down and wait for it to pass.

The dim moonlight seemed blinding. I squinted at the beast beside me. As my vision cleared and my eyes adjusted, I focused on the creature, which I realized was a gorilla.

"Oh my . . . ," I whispered.

Having a giant gorilla loom over you is terrifying, but slightly less terrifying than the Bayport Beast. At least gorillas are real.

The gorilla cocked his head at me and slowly extended an arm. I flinched but stopped myself before another quick movement started that jackhammer in my brain again. The huge primate moved his hand toward me and extended a finger to my forehead. The finger was the size of a kielbasa sausage, but its touch was as gentle as a butterfly. I exhaled as the creature pulled the finger back to his face. The primate sniffed the tiny patch of blood on his fingertip.

"Yeah, that wasn't you," I said, remembering how I had gotten into a fight with a tree and lost.

If this gorilla had wanted to hurt me, he could've tossed my unconscious body around like a rag doll. That made me a little more confident about my safety.

Then I heard a belch behind me. I turned (slowly this time) to see a large orangutan. He had stringy reddish hair and protruding lips. His long arms were crossed, and he seemed to look at me with disapproval.

"What the . . . ," I said, taken aback by the sight of the second primate. "How did you two get here?"

The orangutan sniffed and looked away. I guess he wasn't as much of a people person as the gorilla.

I patted the pockets of my cargo pants and pulled out a couple of protein bars. I peeled the wrapper off one and offered it to the gorilla. The great ape took it from my hand, gave it a sniff, and popped the entire thing into his mouth. Then he did something that was kind of freaky; he thanked me. But he didn't thank me with words (my head injury wasn't *that* severe). He brought his open hand to his mouth and brought it forward in an arc. I knew hardly any sign language, but I knew that that was the sign for "thank you."

"Uh, you're welcome," I replied.

The other bar was snatched from my hand. I turned to see the orangutan shove the entire thing into his mouth, wrapper and all. He gave me a curt "thank you" with one hand before looking away.

"Uh, I was going to open it for you," I said. "It probably doesn't taste as good that way."

The ape chewed briskly for a while before reaching up to his mouth. He slowly slid a slimy, empty wrapper out from between his lips.

"Okay," I said.

A faint chirp grabbed my attention. I spotted another form leaning up against a nearby tree. It was in a deep shadow, so I hadn't seen it right away. I dug through my pockets for another protein bar as I shuffled toward it. As I neared, I saw it was a chimpanzee. I remembered seeing it before I was knocked out—the gorilla had been crouching over it on the ground. I hadn't recognized what it was because it was completely hairless.

"What happened to you, little guy?" I asked. "And . . . where's your hair?"

I unwrapped the protein bar and handed it to the chimp. He took it but not as eagerly as the other two. He seemed tired and weak. I leaned forward and noticed that his left arm was covered with blood.

"Oh, man," I whispered.

I pulled out my phone. I had to call an ambulance, animal control, or someone who could help the chimp. At the very least I could call Joe and have him bring me the first aid kit from my backpack. Unfortunately, my phone didn't have a signal.

"I guess we'll have to bring you to the first aid kit," I told the chimp.

I didn't know exactly what I was working with here, but at least two out of the three apes knew some sign language. That meant they had to be somewhat trained. Hopefully, that meant they could understand some English.

I picked up an empty protein bar wrapper and stood up. "I have more of these," I said, shaking the wrapper. I motioned for them to follow. "Come." I took a couple of steps away from them. "Come on."

The gorilla and orangutan exchanged a look but stayed put. I shook the wrapper again for good measure and took another step back.

Finally the gorilla stood. He lumbered over to the chimpanzee and gingerly scooped it up. He cradled the chimp as he began to follow me. The orangutan blew a long raspberry before finally giving in and coming along.

Great. I got everyone moving. I was the leader of a surreal primate parade. Now I needed to figure out where to go.

IN DEEP 14

JOE

"SIT DOWN AND SHUT UP," JOHANSSON ordered.

Benny and I did as we were told. We sat on the ground next to the folding table, the camp lantern bathing us in golden light. Benny sat beside me, brown face paint surrounding his eyes; he still wore the top half of his Bayport Beast costume. The lower half was still back at the clearing, stuck in the bear trap. Johansson had ordered him to rip it off and leave it behind. Normally seeing Benny sitting there—hairy beast up top, skinny legs and boxer shorts down below—would have been funny. Unfortunately, a man with a rifle tends to suck the humor right out of any situation.

"What are you kids doing out here?" Johansson asked.

"What we said we were going to do," I replied. "We were hunting for the Bayport Beast."

Johansson nodded at Benny. "And him?"

Anger bubbled inside me. "You mean the guy you almost shot?" I asked.

Luckily, back in the clearing, I had reached Johansson just in time, slamming against him as he fired the rifle. Johansson's shot went astray and barely missed Benny.

Johansson resumed pacing. "You were supposed to stay on the lower trails," he said, seemingly more to himself than to us. "You're not supposed to be here!"

"And you weren't supposed to be a *literal* Bigfoot hunter," I barked.

"I can fix this. I can fix this," the man said. "It's my mess, I can clean it up."

"What's he talking about?" Benny whispered.

"I have no idea," I replied.

But what I *did* know was that it was a bad idea to provoke a man with a high-powered rifle. I needed to find out about my brother, and being held at gunpoint wasn't going to get me answers. I had to talk to this guy with a less accusatory tone.

I turned back to Johansson and slowly raised my hands. "Look, maybe we can help. All right?"

The man whipped the rifle around and aimed it at me. "Don't you move!" he ordered.

"I'm not, I'm not," I replied. "I just want to help. But maybe you can help me first. Where is Frank?"

Johansson looked perplexed. "What?"

"Did you do anything to Frank?" I asked.

Johansson squinted and shook his head. "Who?"

"Frank," I repeated. "My brother. Did you do something to him?"

The man glanced over his shoulder. "He's here too?"

"What do you mean?" Benny asked me.

"I found his flashlight near a pool of blood," I explained.

Benny gasped. "What?"

I glared up at Johansson. "You're the only one with a gun out here. What did you do?"

Johansson lowered his rifle and began pacing again. "They got him," he muttered. "Oh no, they got him. But . . . but that's good."

"Who got him?" I asked. "What are you talking about?"

"Nobody can find out," the man continued. He massaged the small bandage on his forehead. "I'll lose everything. All gone. All gone."

I was worried about Frank, but it sounded as if Johansson hadn't seen him. I didn't know what he meant by *they*, though. Who else was out here with him? Or maybe he was imagining someone out here trying to get him.

Benny nudged me. "Dude, he is losing it," he whispered. "This is not good."

Benny was right. Johansson seemed far from the picture of mental health. I had to find my brother, but Benny and I had to get away from Johansson first.

"I'll distract him and you run for it," I whi[s] clear and call 911."

"No way, man," Benny said quietly. "My ph[one] at our campsite." He pointed down. "No pants, [re]member?"

I sighed. "All right, I'll go."

"No one was supposed to find out," Johansson murmured. "No one *can* find out."

I didn't like the idea of leaving my friend alone with an armed madman. But we had to get help before Johansson snapped. It didn't sound like he wanted any witnesses to whatever it was he was doing out here. If we didn't get help soon, I had a feeling neither of us would make it out alive.

Unfortunately, we didn't have a chance to put our plan into action. Johansson aimed the rifle at us. "Stand up," he ordered.

Benny and I slowly got to our feet. "Look," I told him. "We can help you fix whatever problem you have, Mr. Johansson."

"You are going to help me fix it, all right," the man replied. He nodded at the pick and shovel on the ground. "Pick those up."

Benny and I exchanged a glance. "What?" I asked.

He jabbed the rifle in our direction. "I said pick them up!" he barked.

We did as we were told. Benny grabbed the pick and I got the shovel. Johansson stepped aside and motioned for us to walk past him. "Over here."

We moved to an open patch of earth in front of his encampment. The man nodded at the clear space. "Now dig."

I didn't like where this was going. "What for?" I asked.

The man stepped back and raised the rifle. He aimed it directly at my forehead. "I said dig!"

Fear knotted my stomach. If this guy didn't want any witnesses, I had the feeling Benny and I were supposed to dig our own graves.

BROTHER TROUBLE

15

FRANK

I HAD NO IDEA HOW FAR WE WERE FROM OUR campsite. Fortunately, I had my compass and I could just make out a couple of the surrounding hilltops through the moonlit trees. Once I had landmarks, I was able to lead the apes toward the nearest hiking trail. From there, it was an easy hike back to our campsite.

I checked my watch; it was almost three a.m. I hoped Benny had finished scaring the other campers and made it back to camp. If so, both he and my brother were in for the shock of their lives.

"Joe," I said as our odd group moved toward the tents. "Come out of the tent slowly, and whatever you do, don't freak out, okay?"

There wasn't any answer. When I peeked inside the tents, my brother was gone.

A rustling of leaves drew away my attention. I turned to see the orangutan hopping up, trying to reach the food bag we'd hung from a high branch. The technique was meant to keep bears from ransacking one's camp in search of food. I don't think it would've been ape-proof, however. The orangutan batted the bottom of the suspended sack with his fingertips. A couple more jumps and he would've had it.

"That's right," I said. "I promised you dinner."

I moved to the tree trunk and untied the thin cord suspending the bag. The line slid over the branch and the bag dropped into the orangutan's waiting arms. The ape shook the bag, then upended it. Power bars and foil packs of dehydrated meals spilled to the ground like prizes from a camping piñata.

While the orangutan and gorilla tore into the packs, I rummaged through my backpack and retrieved my first aid kit. I attended the hairless chimpanzee while the others popped dried meatballs into their mouths as if they were popcorn.

I knelt beside the chimp and got to work. When I wiped away most of the fresh blood, I saw a small hole in the ape's bicep. "Did someone shoot you?" I asked as I gingerly raised his arm to examine it more closely. There was an exit wound on the other side; the bullet had passed straight through.

I didn't risk cleaning the wound too much. Chimpanzees

were known for their uncanny strength, and the last thing I wanted was to cause the ape pain only to have it send me flying into another tree. I was done slamming my head into trees, thank you very much.

After I'd cleaned the wound as much as I dared, I pulled out some gauze pads and cautiously dressed it. Once the pads were in place, I wrapped a long bandage around the chimp's bicep to keep them in place. That would stop the bleeding for the time being.

I smiled down at him. "We're almost done."

The chimp seemed to sense my intentions; he not only let me handle his wounded arm but raised his other arm and placed a gentle hand against my face.

"What have you got there?" I asked, noticing something on his arm. A series of eight numbers were tattooed on the inside of his right arm.

The chimpanzee didn't answer, of course. Instead, he lowered his arm and closed his eyes. His chest rose and fell slowly as he slept.

With the ape's head tilted back, I noticed a hard plastic collar encircling his neck. I switched on my flashlight and leaned closer. There were three tiny buckles holding the collar closed. No doubt they were meant to be too small for the chimp's thick fingers—but not too small for mine. I carefully unsnapped the buckles and slid the collar from around his neck.

As I examined the collar, I saw a small black box. A tiny

red light pulsed on its side and a logo adorned the top of the box: an upside-down triangle surrounding a flagpole with two pointed flags on either side. A spring encircled the bottom of the pole. It was the same logo from Johansson's business card.

I glanced back at the sleeping hairless chimpanzee, the gorilla and orangutan who knew sign language. They both had similar collars around their necks. Suddenly the logo made perfect sense.

BANG!

A shot rang out in the forest. I thought I'd imagined the one I had heard earlier, but this one was real . . . and it sounded close.

I glanced at our empty tent. My brother was missing, and now there was a gunshot in the woods. Because Joe was . . . Joe, it wouldn't be a stretch to imagine that if there was trouble, he'd be smack in the middle of it. So I did what you're never supposed to do; I ran toward the sound of gunfire.

INCOMING! 16

JOE

ENNY AND I HUGGED THE GROUND. My heart raced as Johansson loomed above us, smoking gun in hand.

"That was your only warning shot," Johansson threatened. The rifle barrel swayed back and forth, from me to Benny. "Now, get up and dig."

We stood and silently grabbed our dropped pick and shovel. Benny swung the pick and I began slicing the ground with the shovel. The ground was soft; we'd have this hole dug in no time.

Part of me hoped that the campers Frank had met would investigate the rifle shot, but I didn't think there was any chance of that. After all, who would be stupid enough to run toward the sound of gunfire? And I wouldn't want any of

95

them to be trapped in this mess with us. Oh, well. Maybe at least they'd call the cops.

"You can't do this," I said, trying to buy us some time.

"Shut it," Johansson ordered.

"I'm a detective, remember?" I asked. "You'll get caught. There's too much evidence connecting you to the scene."

He eyed me suspiciously. "What evidence?"

"All the people who saw you talking to us," I said. "If we disappear, the cops will come to you first."

Johansson sneered. "No one saw us talking."

"Our comic shop has security cameras," Benny added. "You're all over those."

The man's eyes widened and his rifle drooped a bit. "You're lying."

Benny shook his head. "No, I'm not. You'd be surprised how many kids swipe comics."

"Speaking of cameras." I stopped digging. "Remember those five game cameras you bought?"

Johansson's eyes narrowed. "You didn't."

More confident, I leaned on the shovel. "We mounted them all around here. I'm sure you're on a couple of them at least." I didn't mention that one of the cameras was smashed and out of commission.

"You weren't supposed to place them up here," Johansson growled. "I told you to put them on the lower trails."

"Yeah, you *knew* we were going on a Bayport Beast hunt," I said. "So, instead of trying to stop us, which would have seemed very suspicious to a couple of detectives like ourselves, you tried to keep us at the other end of the trail system. Isn't that right?" I asked. "So we wouldn't catch you hunting up here?"

Johansson blinked, overwhelmed. "Yes, but . . . I . . ."

I cocked my head. "And just what were you hunting, anyway? It's sure not the Bayport Beast, because that title belongs to my friend here." I placed a hand on Benny's shoulder. "Dude. You can stop digging now."

Johansson's lips tightened. "That's none of your business." He glanced at Benny. "Keep digging!"

I let the shovel drop to the ground. "Look, you let us go and we'll promise not to turn those cameras over to the police."

"I have a counteroffer," Johansson sneered. "You take me to all those cameras and I won't shoot your friend here." He aimed the rifle at Benny's chest.

Okay, not a big fan of that counteroffer.

A beep came from behind us. A light flashed on the radio on the camp table. Keeping the rifle trained on us, Johansson sidestepped to the table.

"What's that?" I asked.

"I thought the batteries were dead," he muttered.

"Batteries?" Benny asked. "For what?"

"For this," said a voice. Frank stepped out of the woods and into the lantern light. He held out a strip of flat plastic with a black box attached.

The radio beeped louder as Frank approached. He seemed to be holding some sort of tracking device and Johansson had the receiver.

Startled, Johansson aimed the rifle at my brother. "Where did you get that?"

"Off one of your test subjects," Frank said. "The one you shot."

"Test subjects?" I asked.

"Mr. Johansson isn't after the Bayport Beast," Frank said. He narrowed his eyes at the man. "Or maybe it's *Doctor* Johansson? It all came together when I saw the condition of one of your test subjects and then this." He tossed the strip of plastic to me.

It had the same logo that was on Johansson's business card.

"That's not a logo for his production company," Frank explained. "Look at it closely. Remind you of anything? Looks like a modern take on a caduceus, doesn't it?"

My brother was right. The caduceus was an ancient Greek symbol commonly used by the medical field. The original icon has a staff with a feathered wing on opposite sides. Two snakes entwine the staff and face each other. The logo on the box did look like a simplified version.

"It's for my company, Rex Pharmaceuticals. I don't work in TV." Johansson lowered the rifle and rubbed his forehead. "Johansson isn't even my real name. It's Michael Rex. My company is small, and we were already under federal investigation." His lips tightened. "I think someone leaked that we were running trials on primates without authorization." He stumbled to the chair at the table. "After that, I had to do something. . . . I put every penny I had into this company, and we needed to bring a successful drug to market in order to stay afloat. We were at a dead end." He waved a hand at Frank. "You saw the one. It lost all its hair. The drug was a failure."

"What drug?" I asked.

The man shook his head. "It doesn't matter. I was about to be exposed. My career would be over, my company finished; I would lose everything. Everything." Johansson—or Rex—let out a long breath. "I needed to destroy the evidence connecting me to those trials. I was on my way to do just that when my van ran off the road. All three test subjects escaped into the woods." He turned to us. "I needed you boys to place the cameras that might find them. I just didn't want you near the crash site. It was too dangerous . . . too likely that you'd figure it out."

"That crash!" exclaimed Benny.

"Destroy the evidence," Frank repeated. "As in *kill* them. He's already shot one of them."

"So he's been out here hunting monkeys?" I asked. "That's sick, dude."

Frank raised his eyebrows. "Try bigger."

"Bigger?" I asked.

"Turns out his test subjects are a chimpanzee, a gorilla, and an orangutan," Frank continued.

"What?" Benny and I asked in unison.

Frank nodded. "Sorry. They ate all the spaghetti and meatballs." He turned to Rex. "Look, just give me the rifle and we can call animal control or something. Get all the apes somewhere safe."

"Uh, don't you mean that you already called the authorities and they're on their way?" I asked my brother. He had no idea how crazy this guy was.

Rex sprang to his feet. "Nice try." He raised the rifle and Frank backed away. "I haven't been able to get a signal in these blasted woods. I'm sure you haven't either."

"Different carrier?" I offered.

"And now I know right where those apes are," he said. "The bear traps I placed weren't enough, apparently, but I'll find them."

Frank looked at me. "What's going on?"

"Dude, he's going to shoot us," I said.

"Don't forget the cameras," Benny told Rex.

"Oh, I'll find them," the man barked. "Right after I take care of you and those apes."

Just then something rumbled in the woods, a growl so deep that I actually felt it before I heard it. A giant black shape exploded into the light. It was a gorilla. An actual gorilla! And, boy, was it angry! Breathing hard, it narrowed its eyes and snarled at Rex. I'm guessing it wasn't a big fan of the doctor.

Rex swung the rifle around, but he was too slow. The

giant ape knocked it away with a massive backhand. We all ducked as the rifle flew over our heads before spinning into the forest.

The gorilla let out a roar and charged at Johansson. The man scrambled away and disappeared into the forest, the great ape shuffling after him.

"That had to be the scariest, coolest thing I've ever seen," I said.

Frank ran toward the spot where the gorilla disappeared. "Come on." I started after him.

"Uh, guys!" Benny said behind us.

I skidded to a stop and spun around. Benny was frozen stiff while an orangutan had its arms wrapped around his waist. The ape grinned as it laid his head against Benny's side.

Frank doubled back and took in the scene. "Oh, he's cool," my brother said with a dismissive wave. "Just stay calm until we get back." He spun and disappeared into the forest. I shrugged at Benny before running after my brother.

"Come on, guys!" Benny shouted after us.

"Wow," said Frank as I caught up to him. "The orangutan didn't greet me that way."

"It must be his beast suit," I suggested.

Frank laughed. "Well, Benny did want to be the beast."

It wasn't hard to track Rex and the gorilla. We just followed the sounds of pounding footsteps and snapping tree branches.

"YEEEAAAAAAH!" bellowed Rex.

"Is the gorilla hurting him?" I asked.

Frank poured on the speed. "I hope not."

We followed the shrieks until we came upon the gorilla standing just outside a familiar clearing. Rex was in the center of the clearing about twenty feet away, howling in pain. His ankle was clamped inside one of his own bear traps.

Frank stepped forward, about to enter the ring of trees. I grabbed his arm. "Dude. He probably has more of those things out there. Benny found one earlier."

Frank fell back and looked at the gorilla. "But those traps didn't work on you guys, huh?" he asked the animal. "You're smarter than that." He patted the ape on the shoulder.

I raised an eyebrow. "Oh, really?"

"You have no idea," Frank replied. He turned to the gorilla and signed, "Thank you." The ape huffed and made a sign I could only assume was "You're welcome."

My mouth dropped open.

Frank pulled out his cell. "Come on. Let's find a signal. I think Rex is ready for us to call for help now."

OUTGOING 17

FRANK

WATCHED AS REX WAS HOISTED UP THE STEEP incline. The moaning man was strapped inside a basket that was being hauled up by a truck winch. Paramedics followed through the former crash site. At the top, the dark mountain road was awash in flashing police car and ambulance lights.

By the time Joe and I had climbed to the mountain road, a park ranger had just pulled up. It turned out that the campers at the other site had already called to report the gunshots. Being at the hilltop campsite had its advantages, including better cell reception.

It didn't take long before the woods were swarming with police and park rangers. Joe had given them a full report and had led them to the bear traps, Rex's camp, and all the game cameras.

Luckily, Chief Olaf hadn't been among the responding authorities. Joe and I were relieved that Bayport's chief of police didn't get out of bed in the dead of night to respond to a disturbance in the middle of the woods. Even if it was a somewhat *unusual* disturbance.

I watched everything from afar. Benny and I had stayed deeper in the forest to keep the apes calm. None of the primates seemed ready to escape, though. They were mesmerized by the buzzing activity and flashing lights. That is, the gorilla and the chimp were; the orangutan was fawning over Benny in his beast costume. His long arms were still wrapped tightly around our friend's legs.

"Is he ever going to let go?" Benny whispered.

"Didn't you always want a little brother?" I asked.

After a while, Joe approached with one of the park rangers. The young woman wore a tan-and-green ranger uniform and had long, dark braids pulled back in a ponytail.

"Are you sure it's okay?" she asked my brother.

"Yeah, come on," said Joe. "Just no sudden moves."

The woman stepped into the shadows and gazed at my new friends. "Oh, wow," she whispered. "They're wonderful." She cocked her head when her eyes fell on Benny. "Ben, is that you?"

Benny's head dropped. "Yes, Ms. Mosby."

The ranger looked him up and down. "Why are you dressed like that?" she asked. "And what's with the stuff around your eyes? You look like a raccoon."

"Let me guess." Joe pointed to the ranger. "This is your secret beast contact?"

Benny nodded.

I nudged his arm. "Are you going to tell her or shall I?"

"Tell me what?" Ranger Mosby asked.

"I—I'm dressed as the Bayport Beast," he said. "Or, I was." Benny went on to explain how he had roamed the park in order to drum up interest for the beast and for his new product line.

"Ben Williams, you should be ashamed of yourself." The ranger crossed her arms. "No more tips for you, young man."

"Yeah, I thought so," he replied. "I think I'm done with the Bayport Beast anyway."

The ranger pointed to the orangutan at Benny's side. "I don't think she's done with you."

Joe and I looked at each other. "She?" we asked in unison.

Ranger Mosby nodded and glared at Benny. "And when the people from the primate sanctuary get here, I'm going to tell them they have *four* to pick up."

The ranger left to join the others.

Joe pointed to the road above. "So, the rangers said that Rex's wreck happened a week ago. That means the apes have been roaming the forest since then. But that still doesn't explain all the other sightings over the years. How do you explain those?"

I shrugged. "Bears."

Joe shook his head. "You have no imagination."

My brother was wrong. I peered into the dark woods and imagined two eyes gazing back at me, some lonely creature hidden away, tucked into the shadows, remaining forever unseen. Remaining a mystery.

Maybe what I saw that first day in the woods was one of the escaped apes. It probably was. But then again, maybe it wasn't. Maybe I'd caught a glimpse of the real Bayport Beast.

I smiled. I think my brother was right. It is more fun to live in a world where many of these fantastic creatures might, *just might* exist.

Of course, there's no way I'm telling Joe that. I'd never hear the end of it.